The perfect boy?

A name appeared at the top of Walter's computer screen. SEAN BAXTER.

"Sean Baxter!" I exclaimed.

"Sean Baxter?" Roni repeated. "Do you know him?"

"Not to talk to," I said. "I know who he is, though. He plays oboe in the orchestra."

"Is he cute?" Justine asked.

"Yeah. I guess he is kind of cute," I said. "Dark haired. Serious looking. Wears glasses. Quiet."

"Sounds just right for you, Karen," Ginger said.

"Let me check the compatibility factor," Walter said, tapping in some more commands.

The words appeared on the screen: COMPATIBILITY FACTOR: 9.

"That's incredible," Owen said excitedly.

"What does it mean?" I asked.

"It means that on a scale of one to ten, you and Sean Baxter are ninety percent compatible. An almost perfect match!"

Karen's Perfect Match

The Boyfriend Club ™

Karen's Perfect Match

Janet Quin-Harkin

Rainbow Bridge®
Troll Associates

Library of Congress Cataloging-in Publication Data

Quin-Harkin, Janet.
   Karen's perfect match / by Janet Quin-Harkin
      p. cm.—(The Boyfriend Club : #3)
   Summary: Karen tries to cope with the expectations of her Vietnamese parents as she
and her friends at Phoenix's Alta Mesa High School deal with problems caused when
the Nerds create a computer program to find perfect dates for the girls.
   ISBN 0-8167-3416-X (pbk.)
   [1. High schools—Fiction. 2. Schools—Fiction. 3. Friendship—Fiction.
4. Vietnamese Americans—Fiction.] I. Title. II. Series: Quin-Harkin, Janet.
Boyfriend Club : #3
P27.Q419Kar   1994
[Fic]—dc20   94-14327

Produced by Daniel Weiss Associates, Inc.
33 West 17th Street
New York, New York 10011

Printed in the United States of America.

10 9 8 7 6 5 4 3 2 1

To my mother, who always encouraged me to spread my wings and has become a best friend as well as a mother.

Chapter 1

"Karen, wait up!" Roni's loud voice echoed down the tiled hallway. I waited, feeling as if every pair of eyes in the science hall had to be looking at me. I really liked Roni, but why did she have to be so loud? During the first couple of weeks at Alta Mesa High, she had been pretty quiet—not as quiet as me, of course. But she would never have dared to yell down hallways. Ever since she had met Drew Howard, though, she was a changed person. She had truly blossomed into what I suspected was her real self—a loud, fun extrovert.

Nobody ever seriously dreamed that Roni would get Drew to notice her, even if she did come up with some unique attention-getting ideas, like hitting him on the head with her books and throwing chili all over him. After all, Drew was one of the most popular sophomores at our school and he was already dating Charlene Davies, the prettiest cheerleader on the squad. But I guess miracles happen: Drew did notice Roni. They weren't exactly an item yet, but he had dumped Charlene, at least for the moment. And he had even kissed Roni on a date, which made me jealous enough to kill!

Anyway, Roni was now on cloud nine—maybe even cloud nine and a half. She had a big grin on her face as she dodged through the crowd, her short dark curls bouncing up and down as she ran. She caught up with me, draping an arm over my shoulder as she propelled me forward through the hall. "Hurry. I can't wait to tell you," she said excitedly.

"Tell me what?"

"I've got the greatest news in the world," she said.

"About you and Drew?"

"Sort of." She had a secretive smile on her face.

"So tell me! Don't keep me in suspense any longer."

"I want to tell the others at the same time," she said. "Do you think they'll already be waiting at our tree?"

"Where else?" I asked with a smile. Since the first day of school, the four of us—Ginger, Justine, Roni, and me—had been eating lunch under the same tree every day. We could sit in the shade and watch the world go by. Also, we always knew where to find each other, which was pretty useful in a school as huge as Alta Mesa.

The four of us had been flung together by fate on the first day of school. Roni and Ginger were friends from way back. They had been transferred to this high school when their town was rezoned into the city of Phoenix. They were intimidated by this gigantic high school, but at least they had each other. Justine and I hadn't known *anybody* at Alta Mesa.

Justine had come here from a snobby boarding school in the mountains, and I had spent my first eight years of school wearing plaid uniforms and being bossed around by power-nuns at a Catholic girls' school. Talk about not preparing you for the real world! I could diagram sentences. I could spell perfectly. I could even make pictures of stained-glass windows from cut-up pieces of glossy magazines. But I had no idea how to talk to boys, how to dress, how to put on makeup, or even how to stop myself from being trampled in the hallways—no survival skills for real life at all!

I also had another problem, one that only Roni really understood. I came from a different ethnic background from most of the kids at Alta Mesa. My parents were immigrants from Vietnam, and they still hadn't learned to think like Americans. I, on the other hand, had been born here. I didn't want to think and act as if I were still in the old country—I'd never even been there. But just try explaining that to my parents! I spent my whole life following dumb rules nobody else had to face. Roni was the only one who understood what this was like, because her own parents were from Mexico. They were almost as strict and old-fashioned and unreasonable as mine. In fact, Roni and I had first started talking to each other because of our prehistoric parents—on the first day of school, we were both dressed like pioneer girls, in long, full skirts. It was a bonding experience.

"There they are," Roni said as we came out into the fierce sunlight and spotted our friends under the tree. "Hey, you guys! Wait until you hear this!" she yelled. She still had her arm around my shoulder, and she dragged me toward them so fast I thought I was going to trip.

"You're late. Where have you been?" Ginger asked, frowning. "I had the most delicious apricots, but Justine and I ate them all."

"Pigs," Roni said cheerfully. "Karen was talking to the music teacher and I was talking to a certain super-cute guy . . ."

"Drew even talks to you in school now, in front of

all his friends?" Justine demanded excitedly. "Roni, you have arrived! You've almost completely replaced Charlene as Drew's official girlfriend."

"Almost," Roni said quietly. "I'm not sure he's totally given up on Charlene yet. After all, they did go together for a whole year. That's a long time. Sometimes I think he's just using me to teach her a lesson. But other times I'm sure he really likes me for myself."

"Of course he likes you, Roni," I said. "You should see his face light up when he sees you. It's so romantic."

"Yeah, and Ben turns into Silly Putty every time he sees Ginger," Justine said, rolling her eyes. "Now it's just you and me, Karen. We need to find ourselves two cute guys somehow. We'll have to get the Boyfriend Club to work on it."

We'd started the Boyfriend Club as a joke. After all, there were clubs at school for almost everything else. Why not a club that was dedicated to finding perfect guys for each of us? But all joking aside, the Boyfriend Club seemed to work—Ginger had Ben and Roni had Drew. Okay, those matchups weren't *entirely* because of the Boyfriend Club, but I like to think that we helped!

I looked down at the ground, trying to imagine the Boyfriend Club fixing me up with a cute boy. But the idea was too unreal. I'd never even been on a date in my life. The only guys I'd ever danced with had been a group of nerds at the freshman welcome dance, and I certainly didn't want to repeat that experience in a hurry.

"I think the Boyfriend Club would have to work miracles for me," I said with a sigh.

"Why?" Justine asked. "You're pretty, you're very smart—"

"I have parents who have forbidden me to date until I turn sixteen," I added quickly.

"Sixteen! That *is* unreasonable! They expect you to exist for two more boyless years?" Justine demanded. "We'll just have to educate them, Karen. When you come home with a completely suitable, respectable, intelligent guy, they'll have to agree that you've got good taste and give you their blessing."

"Will you two shut up for a second so I can tell my news before I burst?" Roni interrupted.

"You're getting married next week?" Justine quipped.

"Listen to this," Roni said, ignoring her. "Drew's family owns a cabin up at the lake. He's taking a big group of friends camping there next weekend and we're invited."

"All of us?" Ginger sat up suddenly.

"Sure," Roni said. "He invited me, and then he said to bring any of my friends if I wanted to. It's

14

going to be so cool! We can go waterskiing, and Drew's planning a big barbecue."

"Wow, that sounds fabulous," Justine said. "But I don't know if I have any camping gear—my sleeping bag is over a year old! And what kind of tent do you think I'll need? Should I buy hiking boots? Do I need my own water skis? I hope I have time to go to the sporting goods store before Saturday."

Ginger, Roni, and I looked at each other and laughed. Justine was so spoiled by her rich father that she just didn't think the same way the rest of us did.

"Justine, you really are something else," Ginger said. She turned to Roni. "But what about Charlene? Is she coming, too?"

"I understand that Charlene hates bugs," Roni said with a big grin. "She isn't the outdoor type. It will be perfect—me and Drew sitting by the fire under the stars . . ."

"With all your friends keeping an eye on you!" Ginger said. "You really want us there?"

"Are you kidding? Of course I do!"

I bit my lip nervously. "I'd love to come," I said. "But . . ."

"Not another violin recital?" Ginger asked.

"No, thank goodness. No more recitals until the winter concert," I said. "It's just that my parents might not let me go."

"Why not?" Justine asked, surprised. "What could be more fun and healthy than camping with a group of friends?"

I wrinkled my nose. "They might not think it's fun and healthy," I pointed out. "You didn't mention whether Drew's parents are going to be there."

"His big brother from Arizona State will be there to drive the boat on Sunday," Roni said. "It's a big group of kids. You'll be safe enough."

"You guys don't think your parents will give you a problem about going?" I looked from one excited face to the next.

"Why should they?" Ginger said. "My brother was allowed on Boy Scout camping trips when he was only nine. What could my father object to?"

"Yeah, Karen. What's wrong with a harmless camp-out?" Justine added.

I shook my head. "You don't know my parents," I said. "They'll see it as a group of unsupervised kids, ready to get into all kinds of trouble. You remember how hard it was to get them to let me sleep over at Ginger's house the first time."

"So don't tell them," Justine said, as if I were stupid. "Just say you're sleeping over at my house or Ginger's house. You've done that before."

I shook my head. "I've never exactly lied to them," I said. "I might have twisted the truth a little sometimes, or left out a couple of important facts . . . like I did say I was sleeping at Justine's house when we had that party there. But that wasn't really a lie, because I *was* planning to sleep there. I just didn't mention the party part. But I couldn't tell an outright lie. What if something happened at the lake? They'd never trust me again."

"You have to come or it won't be any fun, Karen," Justine said. "How about if we all go over to your house and tell your parents that we'll take good care of you?"

A big grin spread across Roni's face. "How about if we form a new school club called the Outdoor Girls and tell your parents this is our first wilderness training session?"

I had to laugh, but I knew I couldn't deceive my parents over such a big thing as a camping weekend. Roni, of all people, should have understood that. "I'm surprised your parents aren't giving you a hard time, Roni."

"Things have changed at my house," she said. "Ever since my grandmother came for a visit, my mother and I have gotten a lot closer. My parents understand that it's important to me to fit in at school."

"Maybe it's time to take a stand with your parents, Karen," Justine said. "You have to tell them that it's important for you to do stuff other kids do. You want to have fun at school."

I gave another big sigh. "But they don't see it that way," I said. "They think school is for learning and getting good grades and getting into a good college, not for having fun. They wouldn't care if I didn't have a single friend all through high school."

"Oh, Karen, that can't be true. Nobody's parents are that out of touch," Ginger said.

"It is true," I insisted. "Once at my last school some girl was handing out party invitations in the classroom. It seemed as if everyone got one except me. When I went home that night, I told my mother how bad I felt. I thought she would understand, but all she said was, 'Maybe it's a good thing. You don't need any distractions from your schoolwork and your violin.'"

"How mean!" Justine exclaimed. "I thought my new stepmother was a wicked witch, but your mother sounds just as bad."

Roni reached across and patted my hand. "I understand what you're going through," she said. "You have to find a way to let them see that you're not a child anymore and they can't run your life for you."

I felt dangerously close to tears. It was the first time in my life that I had friends who cared about how I was feeling. "They'll still think I'm a baby when I'm thirty," I said. "That's just the way they are. I guess it's one of the problems of being an only child, as well as coming from my culture."

"But they're trying to live your life for you and that's not right," Ginger said. "It's about time we showed your parents that you've grown up!"

"That's right, Karen," Justine said. "You have to be assertive with them. Tell them it's part of the American culture to give children freedom to make their own decisions—"

"I like that," Roni interrupted. "Part of the American culture. Good thinking."

It sounded pretty good to me, too, and it made sense. After all, I was an American. I had a right to the same sort of life as my friends.

"I'll do it," I said. "I'll go home and have it out with them today." I tried to sound a lot more confident than I felt. The thought of having a showdown with my parents made me feel sick. It wasn't that they yelled or anything. They were just always sure that they were right and I was a silly child.

"Way to go, Karen," Roni said, thumping me on the back. "Call me tonight and let me know how it went."

"I've had enough of this heat," Ginger said, getting up suddenly. "I think I'll go check out the library."

I looked across at Justine and Roni. "What's with her?" I asked as Ginger stalked off. "She hardly said anything all lunch hour."

Roni shrugged. "I don't know. She's been acting

weird for the past few days. I wonder if she's having a problem with Ben."

"I saw her with Ben this morning," Justine said. "They looked as happy and goofy as ever."

"Then I have no idea what's wrong," Roni said. "But it's obvious something's eating her. We better find out what it is."

Chapter 2

The house was quiet as I let myself in. That was no surprise—our house was always quiet. My parents never raised their voices. The TV was always kept at low volume, and the only loud sounds came from my violin. Living in my house was like living in a museum.

As I put my backpack down in the front hall, it struck me how much my house looked like a museum, too: not a thing out of place, furniture all polished, pillows plumped, magazines just so on the coffee table, flower arrangement in the window. It could have been a furniture showroom.

"Mom, I'm home," I called.

"I'm in the kitchen," came her answer.

That wasn't a surprise, either. My mother rarely goes out during the day, except to the store. It's not that she doesn't have any friends. There are other Vietnamese families at our church, but my mother isn't what you'd call a joiner. Neither is my father, which is my bad luck. Both of them always had too much time and energy to spend on me, listening to my violin practice, checking over my homework every night, and talking about the day when I'd play at Carnegie Hall (a day I was pretty sure would never come).

I pushed open the swinging door and went through to the kitchen.

"I made cookies," my mother said. "Your favorite—chocolate chip."

"Thank you."

I sat down to a glass of milk and a plate of cookies. This was an afternoon ritual at our house. I tried to imagine Roni in my kitchen. It was a good thing that I'd grown up quiet. How would my folks have handled a daughter who yelled and laughed like Roni?

"How was school today?" my mother asked. She always said this, and I always replied, "Fine, thank you." But today I didn't. All the way home I had rehearsed what I was going to say until it buzzed through my head like an excited bee.

"Terrific," I said. My mother's head snapped up,

her eyes narrowing as she studied me. "I'm really beginning to feel like I belong at that school, Mother."

"That's good, Karen."

"And I've made such nice friends. You like Roni and Ginger and Justine, don't you?"

"They seem like nice girls," she said guardedly. "Of course, I've only met them for a few minutes. I don't know much about their families."

"Their families are nice, too," I said. "I'm so glad you and Dad decided to send me to school there. In fact, I'm even glad that Dad's landscaping business isn't doing too well at the moment, or I'd be at that boring Catholic high school, wearing a plaid uniform, instead of there."

She looked at me suspiciously now. "Karen, what's going on? You're acting so strange."

"It's called being happy, Mom. For the first time I'm really happy. I have friends who care about me, and life is fun."

"Uh . . . that's good, Karen, but I hope you won't start neglecting your schoolwork. Remember, school is not for having fun. It's for getting good grades."

"Oh, that reminds me. I got an A in English today—the only A in the class." At least I had to thank Sacred Heart for drumming all that grammar into me!

"That's very good. Your father will be pleased."

"And there's something I want you to help me ask Daddy," I said. Divide and conquer—that's what they had told us in history class. If I could get Mom on my side, then Dad would crumble and fall!

"I want to go on a camping trip with my friends this weekend."

"A camping trip?"

"Yeah. I'm so excited, Mom. I've never been camping before."

"I'm sure Daddy wouldn't mind you going camping with your friends, if you get your homework and your practice done first."

"You mean I can go?" This was easier than I had thought! Maybe I had normal parents after all.

"I don't see why not. Which family is taking you with them?"

"It's not exactly one family," I said. "A whole bunch of us are going. I'd be going with Roni and my friends . . ."

"Yes, but who has invited you?"

"Roni."

"So it's Roni's family. I'll call her mother and make sure—"

"Mom, Roni's family isn't going. A friend from school arranged it. It's a big class camping trip, a sort of get-to-know-everyone weekend."

A smile spread across my mother's face. "Oh, so it's a school-sponsored activity."

I was very tempted to nod. It would have made everything simple. She'd be sure to agree to a school-sponsored activity. I'd be home free . . . but I couldn't do it. I couldn't tell my parents an outright lie.

"Not exactly," I said. "The kids are organizing it. Drew's big brother will be there to keep an eye on us, and there's a phone at Drew's cabin . . ."

"Drew?"

"A friend of Roni's. I told you about him. He came to my violin recital."

"The boy in the red sports car?"

"That's the one."

"And he's organizing this weekend?"

"Sort of."

"With no adult supervision?"

"His big brother who's in college—"

She was already shaking her head. "I'm sorry, Karen, but you're not going."

"Mom!"

"A group of children with no adults present? I'm sure they'll bring beer and get drunk . . ."

"Mom, listen to me," I said. "Even if some kids bring beer, I won't drink it. I've already promised you I won't drink. My friends and I are normal, sensible girls. We just want to sleep under the stars, and swim, and have fun, okay?"

"No, not okay."

I could feel my throat tightening up and tears stinging my eyes. This was turning out the way it always did—my mother being calm and thinking she was totally right, and me being childish and wrong.

"But why? Why can't you trust me? You've brought me up well. I've never given you any reason to think I'm a bad kid. Why can't you just let me be normal for once?"

Mom was shaking her head while I spoke. "I'm sorry, Karen. American parents might let their children go running off into the wilderness alone, but not where we come from."

"Well, I don't come from where you come from!" I yelled. I don't think I had ever really yelled at my mother before. She looked at me, openmouthed.

Then she said, "Karen, go to your room. You've only been in that school for one month and you're already getting rude and undisciplined like the worst American children."

"And another thing," I said. "I'm not a child anymore. I'm a young person with a right to make my own decisions."

I stalked to my room and slammed the door. Talking to my parents was like talking to a brick wall. They weren't even prepared to listen. I'd never be able to be a normal person, leading a normal life like everyone else. They'd probably come live in my dorm room at college with me, if they even let me go away to college.

I went across to my bed and curled up on it, hugging my knees to my chest. *It's so unfair,* I thought. *I should do like Justine said and tell them to butt out of my life.* After all, what could they do to me? Lock me in my room until I turned twenty-one? But I knew I could never say something like that to them. Ever since I was born, I'd had respect drummed into me—respect for parents, respect for elders, respect for ancestors. If you behaved badly, you let your family and your ancestors down. I felt like I was walking around with a heavy weight of ancestors sitting on my shoulders.

I turned over and lay on my back, staring at the ceiling. I wanted to go with my friends so much, but I didn't know what to say to make my mother change her mind. I should have known she'd never agree to my going away unsupervised for an overnight camping trip. It wasn't something my parents had done in Vietnam, so my mother would never understand why I should do it here. It would be no use trying to convince my father when he came home. He was even more old-fashioned than Mom was. If he had his way, he would probably have arranged my marriage by now!

I knew that I had to talk to somebody or explode.

Suddenly I remembered that Roni had told me to call her and let her know how things went. I opened my bedroom door and dragged the phone into my room. There was only one phone in our house, and it sat in the front hall. My parents didn't believe in unnecessary chatting on the phone. As far as they were concerned, you called someone when you had something to say, said it quickly, and hung up again.

I closed my door quietly and dialed Roni's number. *Please be there,* I prayed. It was a long way from school to her house. She might not be home yet. Then I heard Roni's unmistakable loud voice on the other end.

"Roni, it's Karen," I said. "I had to talk to you."

"What happened?" I could hear the concern in her voice. I told her everything that had gone on between my mother and me. Once I started talking, I couldn't stop. I just kept on, remembering all the times in my last school when I had been left out of things because of my parents. All my frustrations came spilling out. At last I said, "I'm sorry. You don't want to hear all this stuff."

"Sure I do," Roni said. "That's what friends are for. They're safety valves to stop you from exploding."

"Talk about exploding," I said. "I was about to be splattered all over the walls, I can tell you." I laughed uneasily.

"Look, Karen, I know exactly what you're going through," she said quietly. "I go through the same thing. It's hard to have a home life that's unusual and parents who have different customs and values. But you're not going to change everything in one giant step, you know. Your parents can't change their whole personalities. You have to take it one small step at a time. You've already come a long way since you started school with us."

"How?"

"Well, they let you sleep over at our houses, don't they? It took a lot of work to get to them to agree to that. And they let you go to the dance."

"Thanks for nothing," I said, laughing. The dance had turned out to be one of the most embarrassing experiences of my life.

"I know you wish they'd forbidden you to do that," Roni said, laughing with me. "But now we have to work on the next step. Maybe they're not ready for an overnight camping trip yet. After all, that's a pretty grown-up, independent thing to do. I haven't even told my folks about it yet. I'm waiting for a good moment, after we've just finished dinner and everyone's feeling relaxed."

"Roni, are you saying your folks might not let you go, either?"

"I'm hoping they will," she said. "They've been

much more reasonable lately. But you never know. Parents are weird, aren't they?"

"Totally weird, especially mine."

"Still, there's not much we can do about them," Roni said. "I guess we're stuck with them, whether we like it or not."

"I guess so," I said.

"At least we've got each other," Roni said. "Everything seems easier if you know you've got someone who understands."

"You're so right," I said. "I'm really glad I met you, Roni. This last month has been wonderful for me. I feel like a real person for the first time. I had friends at my old school, but there was never anyone I could talk to—not the way I talk to you."

"I guess I've been lucky all my life," Roni said. "I've had Ginger as a friend since kindergarten. We've always shared stuff."

"Roni, you know Ginger better than anyone," I said. "Did you find out why she's acting weird?"

"Nope." She didn't say anything for a few seconds. "I asked her about it on the bus today and she said everything was fine. But I'm not sure I believe her."

"I know what you mean. She looks at me in a funny way sometimes. I'm not even sure she likes me."

"Don't be silly," Roni said. "Everyone likes you, Karen. You're a nice person. Why shouldn't Ginger like you?"

30

"You tell me," I said. "I've never done anything to upset her, but today I caught her giving me such a nasty look, I felt like she wished I would disappear."

Roni laughed. "I'm sure you got it wrong," she said. "Maybe the sun was in her eyes and she was squinting."

"I hope so," I said. "I'd sure hate to upset you guys, after you've been so nice to me."

I heard the front door slam.

"Whoops, gotta go," I whispered. "My dad just came home. No sense in getting in more trouble tonight, or they'll decide that I've turned into a juvenile delinquent!"

I could hear Roni laughing. "You, a juvenile delinquent? That's pretty funny!" she said.

"I can't wait for my father's reaction when he hears I wanted to go on an unsupervised camping trip with boys," I said. "I hope your parents are more reasonable, Roni."

"Of course, I could always lie about this trip," she said. "But I'm like you—I feel bad about deceiving my folks. Just pray that I get them in a good mood."

"I will. Bye, Roni, and thanks for listening."

"Hey, no problem. Anytime you want to talk, I'm here," she said. "Well, I'm off to sprinkle good humor powder in their enchiladas. Bye, Karen."

Chapter

3

The next morning when I arrived at school, I found Roni cramming stuff into her locker, throwing books inside with a terrible clang that echoed up and down the hallway.

"Hi," I said.

"Don't talk to me," she snapped. "I'm not in the best mood."

"Why, what happened?"

"My folks freaked out about the camping trip. Talk about out of touch! Why did I have to be born into such a dumb family?"

"They won't let you go?"

"No," she said, slamming the locker shut. "They refused to even listen. I tried to explain that there would be a big group of us and my friends would be there to keep an eye on me, but do you think they'd try to understand? Nooooo! It was just, 'I'm sorry, Veronica, but you are not going to be alone with a boy when his family isn't there.' Talk about the Dark Ages!"

"I'm really sorry, Roni," I said. "I know how much this meant to you."

"Drew will think I'm totally lame," she said, turning to me with a despairing look. "I bet there will be lots of gorgeous girls there, all waiting for Drew to give them water-skiing lessons. 'Oh, Drew, I can't seem to get the hang of this. Put your arms around me and show me again.' He probably won't remember who I am by the time he gets back."

"Of course he will," I said. "He'll understand. If your family is strict, there's not much you can do about it."

"I know," she said with a big sigh, "but I was really hoping that they were finally going to act like normal parents."

"I bet Ginger and Justine will be disappointed," I said. "I'm sure their parents didn't think it was any big thing to want to go camping with their friends."

I had hardly finished talking when I noticed Ginger stalking down the hallway. "And furthermore, I'm *not* a little kid and you don't own me!"

she was yelling at somebody over her shoulder.

"What was that all about?" Roni asked her, giving me a worried look.

"My dumb brother and that stupid idiot Ben," Ginger said.

"Ben said something to upset you?" Roni asked. "I thought Ben was perfect in every way."

"He was, until now," Ginger snapped. "I didn't say anything about the camping weekend to my dad yet, because I thought he might not like the idea. But Todd and Ben heard about it from some guys on the football team, and they both had a fit. Todd said he heard there's going to be some wild stuff up there—you know, a lot of partying—and he's going to tell Dad that I shouldn't go. And Ben kept telling me that they weren't my kind of kids and I wouldn't have a good time, which just annoyed me more. How does he know what my kind of kids are?"

Roni and I looked at each other and grinned.

"What's so funny?" Ginger demanded. "You look like you're glad I'm not allowed to come."

"It's not that," Roni said.

"Then what?"

"It's just that . . ." Roni glanced across at me again and giggled. "Karen and I can't go, either."

"Really?" Ginger's eyes opened wide. "Your folks won't let you go, Roni?"

"I tried," Roni said. "Believe me, I tried every way I knew. I cried. I had a temper tantrum. I told them they were wrecking my life and that I was going to lose the one adorable boyfriend I'd ever have in my entire life and I'd probably never get married and they'd have to support me until I turned fifty, but nothing worked. They just said that I was too young to go off on my own for a weekend. Period."

"Mine said the same thing," I added.

Ginger looked from Roni to me. "Well, so much for all the fantastic plans we were making yesterday," she said. "There's just one small problem."

"What?" I asked.

"Justine. I bet she's already bought a thousand dollars' worth of camping equipment and had a couple of water-skiing lessons. She's going to be so mad—"

"Here she comes now," I said. Justine was running down the hall toward us.

"You won't believe this," she called as soon as she was close enough. "They're ruining my whole life!"

"Who?" Roni asked.

"My father and stepmother, of course. Or should I say my father and the Wicked Witch of the West?"

"What did they do?"

"They won't let me go on the camping trip," Justine said. "I asked for money at dinner last night. I just said that I needed a couple of hundred to equip myself for the weekend, and they wanted to know what for! And when I told them, the Wicked Witch said I wasn't going on any camping trip without adults present and my dad agreed with her. I'm sorry, guys. I guess you're going to have to go without me."

Roni and Ginger and I burst out laughing.

"You're glad I'm not coming with you?" Justine demanded angrily.

"No, Justine. We have to laugh, or we'd all be crying," Roni said. "None of us can go, either. All our families freaked out at the idea."

"I suppose I can understand it, really," Ginger added. "I mean, if it's going to be a football team thing with lots of drinking, then we probably shouldn't be there. All sorts of things could go wrong. People could start fires by accident, or fall in the lake, or crash the boat. I can understand why our parents were worried."

"I suppose I can, too," Roni said. "Maybe I am a little young to go running off for the weekend with my boyfriend. Oh, well. I guess we're stuck sleeping over at one of our houses again."

"We could sleep over at mine," Justine said. "Hey, I know. We could camp out in my backyard. We could sleep out next to the pool and pretend it was the lake."

"That sounds better than being at the lake with a

lot of beer-drinking guys acting loud and stupid," Ginger said.

"We'll have more fun on our own!" Justine cried.

"Except Drew won't be there," Roni said softly. "He'll be up at the lake acting like Mr. Wonderful to all the other girls."

"At least Charlene's not going," I said. "And I bet a lot of her friends won't go, either—they're probably all afraid of bugs."

"Now that you mention it," Justine said, "I think I prefer sleeping in my backyard to being out in the wilderness where all sorts of slimy, creepy things can pop out of nowhere at any moment—"

"Hello, girls!" said a squeaky voice right behind us. We looked up to find ourselves standing in a circle of nerds.

The nerds were about as scary as freshman guys can get. They always hung around us, obviously hoping to charm us with their creepy smiles. Unfortunately, we were all too softhearted to tell them to get lost, like most of the other kids did. I kind of felt sorry for them. People were constantly making fun of them and were totally rude to them. Being new at Alta Mesa ourselves, we knew what it was like to be outsiders. So we tolerated the nerds—we just tried to stay out of their way as much as possible.

The trouble was that they had this unnerving habit of appearing out of nowhere. We'd be sitting under our tree and suddenly there they were, all around us. Other kids walked noisily down the path. Nerds crept silently. It was very scary and really unfair. They didn't give us a chance to escape.

This was exactly what had happened now. The nerds were in a circle around us, pinning us against our lockers, grinning their ghastly grins.

"So, girls, can we expect the pleasure of your company today?" Owen asked. He was the shrimpy one with the squeaky voice and the spiky hair.

"Today?" We looked at each other desperately.

"Yes. Need we remind you that today is Wednesday?" Ronald said. He was the serious one, tall as a beanpole.

"Oh, good, Wednesday," Ginger said.

"That's right! Computer Club day," Walter said excitedly, switching his briefcase from one hand to the other.

"Remember you thought you couldn't come because it clashed with the Ballet Club, Roni?" Owen said, blinking rapidly at her. "Well, we happened to check and we found out there is no Ballet Club. You must have confused it with the Badminton Club, and that's on Thursday."

"Oh, no," Roni said. "I meant Ballet Club. I was trying

to get one started. I'm just dying to dance *Swan Lake*."

I started giggling, imagining Roni leaping across the stage in a tutu. Next to me I could see Justine fighting to keep a straight face, too.

"Maybe we could help you get it started," Ronald said. "I did some ballet once myself."

"You did?" Roni shot me a horrified glance.

"Yes, when I was about four. My mother wanted to stop me from falling over my feet so much, so she enrolled me in ballet. I wasn't very good at it, if I remember correctly, but I'd be prepared to give it another try to help you out."

I was trying to picture Ronald in white tights, leaping across the stage and lifting Roni above his head. Roni must have been thinking the same thing, because she said hastily, "That's very nice of you, Ronald, but I've decided to wait awhile. *Swan Lake* takes up so much time . . ."

"That's great," Walter said, exchanging delighted glances with Wolfgang. Wolfgang was the strong, silent one. He weighed about three hundred pounds, always wore a purple sweater with a brown stag on it, and didn't say much. "Now there's nothing to stop you girls from coming to the Computer Club today! We have something special to show you."

"You've created a female android?" Justine asked, wrinkling her nose.

"That's very funny, Justine," Owen said. "The concept of the android—that is, a humanoid form that is machine generated—is still beyond the power of computer science. However, we at the Alta Mesa Computer Club like to think that we are helping humanity in our own small way—"

"Which should be of special interest to you girls," Ronald interrupted, "seeing that you have your Boyfriend Club."

"Our what?" We were looking at them in horror. We had thought that the Boyfriend Club was our own little secret. How did these guys hear about it?

"It is our understanding that you are all members of a Boyfriend Club," Walter said, nodding seriously, "the object of which is to help each other get dates."

"Who told you that?" Ginger demanded.

"We . . . sort of . . . overheard," Ronald confessed.

"You spied on us?" Justine gasped.

"I wouldn't put it that way," Ronald said. "We just happened to be following you girls and overheard you talking about your club. But please don't worry. Your secret will be safe with us."

"In fact," Walter said, "we've been working very hard on your behalf. We actually devoted the last meeting of the Computer Club to making life easier for you."

"Walter, what are you talking about?" Roni demanded.

Walter blushed. "We've created a program for you," he said.

"What kind of program?" Justine asked.

"To come up with a perfect match," Owen said proudly. "We've entered the information on hundreds of guys into our database, including whether they're available or not. Now all we have to do is feed in *your* information and bingo! We fix you up with the perfect guy."

We weren't giggling anymore.

"Are you serious?" Justine asked.

"Come at lunchtime and you'll see," Ronald said. "I think you'll be impressed. Walter is really hot stuff with databases."

"I've been dabbling since I was six years old," Walter said modestly.

"Are you sure this thing isn't rigged so that it fixes us up with you guys?" Justine asked suspiciously.

"Certainly not," Owen said. "We're serious scientists. We don't rig our experiments."

"So you'll come at lunchtime?" Ronald asked.

We looked at each other, then nodded. "We'll be there," Ginger said.

"Then we'll see you in the computer room, twelve-thirty sharp," Owen said. "Who knows, maybe you'll leave with the guy of your dreams."

They moved off down the hall as the bell rang for first period.

"Tell me if I'm wrong," Ginger said, "but did I actually just agree to spend my lunch hour with the nerds?"

"You did."

"Are we crazy? Do we want to be locked in a room with them?" Ginger demanded.

"I know it's a scary thought," Justine said, "but maybe it's worth the risk. They might be onto something here, Ginger. It's okay for you. You've got Ben and Roni's got Drew . . ."

"Maybe not, after this weekend," Roni said with a frown.

"But Karen and I need to meet guys. Maybe the nerds really *will* fix us up with the dates of our dreams."

"Dates of your nightmares, if I know the nerds," Roni said.

"Well, I think it's worth a try. Don't you, Karen?" Justine asked.

I nodded. "It's *definitely* worth a try," I said.

Chapter

4

"If this doesn't wreck our reputation forever, I don't know what will," Roni muttered as we walked to the computer lab at lunchtime. "What do you bet that Charlene or Drew comes down the hall as we emerge, surrounded by nerds?"

"You don't have to come if you don't want to," Justine told her. "You've already found the cutest guy in the school without the help of computer matching."

Roni grinned. "Yeah, I did it the old-fashioned way—hit him with a French book and then threw chili at him," she said.

"And then had him throw ice cream at you," Ginger added. "All in all, it's been a romantic friendship so far."

"Don't knock it until you've tried it," Roni said with a big, self-satisfied smirk. Then a worried look clouded her face. "I just hope he still remembers who I am by Monday morning."

"Did you tell him that you couldn't go on the camping trip yet?" Ginger asked.

"Yes," Roni replied.

"And what did he say?"

"He was really nice," Roni said. "He said not to worry about it, that it was no big deal. I just hope he meant it. And I hope Charlene doesn't suddenly decide that she likes bugs." Roni sighed, then managed a smile. "I bet there's nobody as cute as Drew in that database. I bet it's a whole database full of nerds."

Justine and I shot each other worried looks. "You don't really think so, do you?" I asked.

"I'll tell you one thing," Justine said. "I intend to check out any guy who comes out of their computer list before I agree to meet him. They might not even know any normal guys."

A whole list of nerds! I shuddered. All morning I had been excited. I knew it wasn't very probable that the nerds could fix me up with the guy of my dreams, but I guess I'm a romantic at heart. I wanted to believe that something really special was going to happen. In fact, I'd almost convinced myself that today was going to be my lucky day. But I tried not to let the others know how excited I was feeling, because they seemed to be taking the whole thing pretty much as a joke.

I guess Roni noticed that I was being unusually quiet. "Look, Karen," she said, "you don't have to do this if you don't want to. I know that having the nerds find you a date might be embarrassing for you."

"Oh, no, I'll come along with you guys," I said lightly. "It might be kind of fun to see who they come up with."

"They can run their compatibility program on Drew and me," Roni said. "I wonder if we'll come out as soul mates."

"What if you don't?" Justine asked. "Wouldn't it be terrible if the program said you were totally unsuited for each other?"

"Then I'd believe the program was no good," Roni said easily. "Here we are! At least we made it to the computer lab without being seen."

We all looked at the door for a minute. Finally, Justine took a deep breath and pushed it open.

"Come on in, girls," Owen called cheerfully. "We've got everything up and running." They were standing there in a line, as if they'd been waiting for us.

"Who wants to be first?" Walter asked, seating himself at the computer.

Justine looked at me. "You go first," I told her.

"Okay, Justine," Walter said, his hands poised above the keyboard, "tell me the personal characteristics that you'd like me to input."

"Let's see," Justine said thoughtfully. "Gorgeous, athletic, rich, fun, blond . . ."

"And what sort of interests?" Walter asked.

"Let's see . . . skydiving—"

"Skydiving?" Roni shrieked. "Justine, when have you ever been skydiving?"

"I didn't say I'd ever done it, but I'd kind of like to try it. Besides, I want to make sure I meet adventurous guys."

"What other interests?" Walter pressed her.

"There are so many fun, exotic things I've done," Justine said. "Let's see . . . foreign travel, white-water rafting, tennis camp, skiing, ballet dancing—no, scrub the ballet dancing. I don't want to be matched up with a wimp."

"How about mud wrestling, then?" Roni quipped.

Justine scowled at her. "I don't want a mindless jock, either," she said. "I suppose I need something sensitive in there, too. How about music—"

"And what things are you looking for in a guy?" Walter interrupted before Justine could fill up the entire screen with her interests.

"Oh, that's easy," Justine said, tossing back her blond ponytail. "He has to be super-cute, with dark hair and blue eyes, over six feet, muscular, a sharp dresser, smart but also athletic, very sensitive, has to drive a sports car . . . very, very rich, because I like lots of money spent on me . . ."

I caught Roni's eye. Was Justine being serious? It was always hard to tell when Justine was putting on an act. She usually got really outrageous when she wasn't very sure of herself. As I watched Justine's face, an amazing thought struck me. Maybe she was afraid that the computer really would come up with a guy for her, and she didn't want it to make a match. That's why she was giving all those impossible requirements.

"You don't want much, do you, Justine?" Ginger asked dryly.

Justine looked surprised. "I might as well go for what I really want," she said. "Why settle for second best?"

"Okay, here goes," Walter said doubtfully. "Let's see what my database can find for you."

He pressed the enter key. The screen went blank while the computer worked. We all held our breath, waiting for the perfect guy to appear on-screen.

At that moment the door opened with a loud creak. The timing was so perfect that everyone gasped. A boy stood in the doorway. He *was* tall and dark, but those were the only two of Justine's requirements he met.

For one thing, he wasn't exactly a sharp dresser. He was wearing baggy jeans held up by rainbow-striped suspenders and a red-and-white-striped rugby shirt. His hair was shaved at the sides but hung down at the back in a long ponytail, and he wore a big, black Indiana Jones hat. The effect was startling, but very definitely weird. He looked almost like a movie villain, except that his face wasn't evil. It was young and sweet. And at the moment, it wore an alarmed expression.

"Oh, sorry," he muttered. "I didn't think anyone would be in here."

"It's Wednesday. Computer Club day," Owen said. "You can join us if you like."

"Oh . . . no thanks," the guy said. "I just needed to run a design, but some other time will do." Then he spun around and practically ran out the door.

"There you are, Justine. You can't say that wasn't rapid service," Ginger said with a laugh.

"I wanted the guy of my dreams, not my nightmares," Justine said. "Who on earth was that?"

"Oh, that's the guy they call Weird Waldo," Owen said. "He's very strange—a real loner. He always dresses like he's in a circus."

"I haven't seen him around," Roni commented.

"No, you wouldn't," Owen replied. "He doesn't go to many regular classes. He's in the gifted program, always doing independent studies. Not exactly your conventional type."

Roni and I exchanged amused glances. This, coming from someone who wore a button-down shirt and polyester pants!

"So he didn't have anything to do with your program?" Justine demanded.

Walter giggled. "Justine, computer programs can't make guys materialize out of thin air," he said. "I can merely supply you with a name. How and when you meet the boy is up to you."

"And what name is your computer coming up with for me?" Justine asked. "There isn't anything on the screen yet."

"That's strange," Walter said. He tapped a few keys. We could hear the computer working, and then three words appeared: NO MATCH FOUND.

"No match found? What is it talking about?" Justine yelled. "I make a perfectly reasonable request and it can't come up with a match for me? What kind of program is this, anyway?"

"I guess the type of guy you described just doesn't go to school here," Roni said. "You were asking the impossible, Justine. Maybe you should try again. Be more reasonable this time."

"Reasonable?" Justine snapped. "What was unreasonable about wanting a cute, intelligent, rich jock?"

"Who also happens to like skydiving and drives a sports car?" I said. "Justine, there aren't too many guys like that at Alta Mesa."

"There aren't too many guys like that, period," Roni agreed.

"Dumb program," Justine sniffed. "I told you they'd only put nerds into their database. I bet all the cute guys refused to have their names entered."

"But we didn't tell anyone we were inputting their names," Walter said. "The list includes every male student who is not currently involved in a steady relationship with a girl. We could try again, Justine. Maybe cut out the skydiving this time."

"No, thanks," Justine said. "I don't compromise. Run it for Karen instead. I'm sure she'll be easy enough to please."

"How about it, Karen?" Walter asked.

"Okay," I said shyly. "Like Justine said, I'm sure I'm easier to please than she was."

"So tell me about yourself first."

"I'm not sure what I'm like. Just ordinary," I said. "Quiet, sort of shy around strangers . . ."

"Fun when you get to know her," Roni added. "Great sense of humor. Fantastic violin player."

"What are you, her PR person?" Justine demanded. She was obviously still mad that the computer hadn't found her perfect boy.

"She's too modest to say good things about herself," Roni said. "I know Karen. You have to push her a little to get her started."

"So I'll put music as a primary interest. Right, Karen?" Walter asked.

"I guess," I said. "Put down all kinds of music. I don't like only classical, you know. I like rock as much as anyone else does."

"What other interests?"

"Reading," I said. "Movies . . . I don't know what else. I don't do much. I must be a boring person."

"No, you're not," Roni said fiercely. "You haven't been allowed to do many things yet because of your music. But you are definitely not boring, Karen."

"What characteristics are you looking for in a guy?" Walter asked.

"Tall, dark, and handsome. What else is there?" Justine cracked.

I smiled. "Sounds good to me," I said. "Nice personality. Easy to talk to. That's all I really want. After all, this will be a first dating opportunity for me. I'm kind of shy around boys."

"But that doesn't mean she wants a real wimpy dork," Roni interrupted. I was glad she'd said that. I would've said it myself, but I thought the nerds might take it personally.

"All right," Walter said. "Let's run it."

The screen went blank. *Okay,* I thought, *it's just like for Justine. There's nobody for me, either.*

Then a name appeared at the top of the screen. SEAN BAXTER.

"Sean Baxter!" I exclaimed.

"Sean Baxter?" Roni repeated. "Do you know him?"

"Not to talk to," I said. "I know who he is, though. He plays oboe in the orchestra."

"Is he cute?" Justine asked.

"Yeah. I guess he is kind of cute," I said. "Dark haired. Serious looking. Wears glasses. Quiet."

"Sounds just right for you, Karen," Ginger said.

"Let me check the compatibility factor," Walter said, tapping in some more commands.

The words appeared on the screen: COMPATIBILITY FACTOR: 9.

"That's incredible," Owen said excitedly.

"What does it mean?" I asked.

"It means that on a scale of one to ten, you and Sean Baxter are ninety percent compatible. An almost perfect match!"

"Wow!" I said. I was trying to picture Sean's face, trying to imagine him as somebody just right for me. I'd only seen him from across the room, among all those other faces in the woodwind section. Had there been anything special about him that I'd noticed subconsciously? Had our eyes met

54

across the sea of faces? Had there been a spark of attraction between us? I couldn't remember. Maybe we'd smiled at each other when the conductor was yelling, but I'd shared a smile with lots of kids in the orchestra during the conductor's famous tantrums.

"So what does Karen do now?" Justine asked impatiently.

"That's up to her," Walter said. "I just match you up with guys. I don't set up the dates."

"That's a lot of help," Justine snapped. "How are we supposed to get her together with Sean? She can't just walk across the orchestra room and say, 'Hi, the computer says we're ninety percent compatible, so how about a date?'"

I laughed nervously. "I can't see myself doing that," I said. "I'd never have the nerve to go up and speak to him out of the blue."

"Of course not," Roni said. "If he's compatible with you, he's probably a little shy, too—he'd be very embarrassed. This is a job for the Boyfriend Club! This is exactly what we started the club for."

"What are you going to do?" I asked quickly. I didn't want Roni walking up to Sean and telling him I was his perfect match!

"First we have to do our research," Roni said. "We find out everything we can about Sean. Then we meet and pool our information and plan how you two can get together."

"And if you need any help from us . . ." Owen suggested.

I tried not to shudder visibly.

"Thanks for the offer, Owen," Roni said. "If we need you, we'll call you." She got to her feet. "Well, guys, we'd better get started."

"What about Justine?" Walter asked. "We still have to run her program again."

"Oh, that's okay," Justine said. "I think I'll see whether Karen's works first. If her date turns out all right, then maybe I'll let you try it again for me. But I think you'll have to expand that database of yours."

"To what?" Ginger asked.

"Aren't there any private schools for rich kids in the area?" Justine asked. "And what about college guys? I obviously need someone more sophisticated and exciting than Alta Mesa can provide."

"Get out of here, Justine," Roni said, giving her a playful push. "College guys! You're a high school freshman. Get real."

"I'm serious," Justine said. "Just because I've led a more interesting life than the rest of you . . ."

Roni, Ginger, and I looked at each other. "Justine, shut up," we said in unison.

Justine turned red and stalked out of the room. I

watched her go, not knowing whether to be annoyed or sympathetic. Justine had that effect on people. Most of the time she acted like a super-confident snob, but every now and then her act slipped, and I got a glimpse of the scared, unsure person inside.

I wondered if Roni and Ginger had noticed this, too. I decided to talk to Roni about it next time I called her. But right now we had other things to think about, like how I was going to meet Sean Baxter, my Mr. Right.

Chapter 5

The next morning at school I was on the lookout for Sean. Maybe we'd bump into each other in the halls and something magical would happen.

But it wasn't Sean I kept running into. It was that other guy, the one they called Weird Waldo. I'd never seen him around school before, but now I kept noticing him everywhere I went. It was like I was being haunted.

As I headed for my locker before first period, I saw a figure running in the opposite direction. I recognized Weird Waldo by the broad-brimmed black hat. This time he was also wearing a long black cape. It streamed out behind him as he ran, making him look like a huge black bat. There was something creepy about the way the cape billowed out. I half expected to see him take off and fly, but he just turned the corner and disappeared.

Then, at midmorning break, I noticed Sean heading for the library. Impulsively I followed him, thinking I would cause a "chance" encounter to make him realize we were destined for each other. But as I hurried around a row of bookshelves in the library, I was suddenly attacked by a black cape! Weird Waldo had climbed up to reach a book on the top shelf and his cape hung out at eye level, brushing my face and making me gasp with alarm. He was so intent on finding his book that he didn't even notice me. By the time my heart had stopped racing, Sean had left the library.

Roni, Ginger, and Justine had told me that I should stay out of their detective work about Sean. They said it wouldn't be right if he found out I'd been snooping and asking questions about him. When we finally got together, our meeting had to seem completely natural and unplanned—as if it was destiny that had brought us together. So I waited impatiently until the Boyfriend Club met for lunch under our tree.

"Okay," Roni said, "I've come up with some good stuff. How about you guys?"

"I didn't find out much," Ginger said. "Sean

doesn't hang out with the football crowd. Todd and Ben didn't even know who he was. All I heard is that he lives over toward Scottsdale."

"Well, I did better than that," Justine said. "I must say, I have a nose for sleuthing."

Roni and I looked at Justine's tiny button nose and started to laugh. "That's because it's not big enough to be much use for anything else, Justine," Roni said.

"Oh, shut up," Justine said, grinning. "It may interest you to know that boys find my nose very cute."

"Don't leave me in suspense any longer—tell us what you found out," I said. "It's my life we're talking about here. My whole future as a normal person."

"Okay. This is what I found out from Ann, who sits in front of me in my new math class," Justine said. "She and Sean went to the same elementary school, so she knows all about him. His mother is a big sponsor of the Scottsdale Symphony. His whole family is into music. He's kind of quiet, but he's nice when you get to know him."

"That sounds perfect for you, Karen!" Roni said.

I nodded. "So how do I meet him?"

Justine looked even more pleased with herself than usual. "I did a little checking in the newspaper, and it turns out that the Scottsdale Symphony is playing this Saturday night. Ann told me that his whole family has season tickets. They attend all the performances."

"Perfect," Roni said. "What could be easier? We go to the symphony and just happen to bump into Sean. You say, 'What a surprise. Imagine meeting you here.' And then you let love take over!"

"It would be even better if we could find out what seats they had and get Karen the seat next to him," Justine suggested.

"If his mother's the president or whatever, they probably have expensive seats," I said, "and they're probably in a block for season ticket holders."

"Wait, Karen, don't you know anybody who's a season ticket holder for the Scottsdale Symphony?" Ginger asked.

I nodded again. "My music teacher plays with the symphony," I said. "I could ask her if she has any extra tickets for Saturday night."

"Great. You even have an excuse for being there," Justine said. "This is going to work really well."

"If I get up the nerve to speak to him," I said.

"One of us should go with you," Roni said firmly.

"How about if we all go? I want to see what happens," Justine said. "I want to be there the moment their eyes meet and he whispers that he's been wanting to talk to her ever since he first saw her."

Roni shook her head. "One of us," she said. "We don't want to scare him away. And it can't be you, Justine. You might say one of your dumb things."

"What dumb things? I don't say dumb things!"

"Yes, you do," Ginger commented. "Who said she wanted to meet someone super-rich because she likes lots of money spent on her?"

"Justine just says stuff like that. She doesn't really mean it," I said.

Justine looked at me in surprise. For a second our eyes met, and I knew I was right about her. I gave her a friendly smile.

"Maybe you should go, Roni," Justine said. "You're not afraid to talk to strange guys. You'll know what to say."

"Okay," Roni said. "If Karen needs a little push, I'd be happy to give it to her."

I looked across at Roni. "I'm glad you're going with me," I said. "I don't think I could face something like this on my own."

"Maybe we could go shopping together first," Roni suggested. "I'll help you choose something special to wear so that you knock him off his feet."

"I've got a great black leather miniskirt—" Justine said.

"Justine," Roni interrupted. "We already know that Sean is quiet and shy. We want to knock him off his feet, not blast him into outer space. Karen has to be herself, but look her prettiest."

"So I guess we won't be having our usual weekly sleepover," Ginger said quietly.

"Why not?" Roni asked. She didn't seem to notice that Ginger's voice was high and tight. "Karen and I will come over to Justine's house after the concert."

"You'll probably be going out with Sean after the concert," Ginger said.

"I don't know if things will get that far," I said, feeling my cheeks turn pink.

"Even if we do go out after the concert, don't you want to find out all the details right away?" Roni asked. "If Justine's folks say it's okay, I vote we come on over to her house. Then we can tell you all that happened while we sit in Justine's hot tub."

"Fine with me," Justine said.

"Ginger?" Roni asked.

"I guess," Ginger said. "If I'm not busy. Ben might want to do something that night."

"I thought he and Todd usually hung out with the guys on Saturday nights," Roni said.

"They do, usually," Ginger said. "But Ben might decide that he'd rather be with me."

"So tell him you do stuff with us on Saturday nights," Justine said. "I don't want to hang around all by myself until Karen and Roni get back from the concert."

"Ginger will be there," Roni said.

"You can read my mind now?" Ginger demanded.

Roni looked surprised. "What's eating you?"

"Nothing," Ginger said. "I guess I'll be there."

"Then it's settled," Roni said. "Operation Karen is under way!"

On Saturday afternoon Roni and I went shopping. I didn't have much money to spend, but Roni went through my wardrobe and decided I'd look fine in the black-and-white outfit I wore for my last violin recital. All we needed to do was jazz it up a little. We found the perfect thing at an accessories boutique in the mall: a big silk sunflower. When we got back to my house, Roni combed my hair up on one side and fixed the sunflower behind my ear. It made my face seem very different. I'd always worn my hair in a straight bob around my face. I hardly recognized myself in the mirror!

"You've got great bone structure," Roni said, looking over my shoulder.

I sucked in my cheeks and decided that this might actually be true.

"All we need is a little eye pencil and blush," Roni said. She got out her cosmetic bag.

"You'd better make it subtle," I said, glancing at my bedroom door. "My mother will have a fit if she thinks I'm going out with makeup on."

"Don't worry. She'll never know." Roni drew a narrow line across the top of my eyes and put some blush on my cheeks.

"Looking good," Roni said, examining her work. "Sean Baxter would have to be crazy if he didn't fall for you right away."

"I hope I can go through with this, Roni." I grabbed her arm. "I'm hopeless when it comes to boys."

"Don't worry about it," Roni said. "I'll be there to get things started, and after that . . . well, you two are ninety percent compatible. I'm sure you'll chatter away nonstop and I'll be left listening to the boring symphony."

"It still seems like a dream to me," I said. "A computer finds me my ideal guy? Me with a boyfriend? *Me?* I never thought it would happen."

"Don't put yourself down, Karen." Roni shook her head. "Any boy would be honored to have you as his girlfriend. You're one of the nicest people I've ever met. You never say anything bad about anybody."

"Well, I think you are *the* nicest person I've ever met," I told her. "I could never talk to anybody the way I talk to you. I'm so glad you're coming with me tonight."

Roni grinned. "Yeah, imagine if it was Justine," she said. "She'd probably blow the whole thing by telling Sean's mother that personally, she'd rather fly to Vienna for the symphony than bother with this provincial stuff."

I laughed. "Poor Justine," I said.

"Poor? Don't you mean rich Justine?"

"I feel sorry for her," I said. "I mean, she has to put on this phony snobby act just because she's not comfortable with herself the way she really is."

Roni looked interested. "Do you think so?"

"I'm sure of it," I said. "Whenever she doesn't know how to act, she starts bragging about herself. I noticed that the other day when we were computer matching."

"Maybe you're right," Roni said thoughtfully. "I guess deep down, she's insecure. I suppose I should try to be more understanding. But you have to admit, she can be a pain sometimes."

"She sure can," I agreed, laughing. "But I think we're whipping her into shape. Especially now that she knows we're her friends."

Roni nodded. "I bet she's never had real friends before."

"I know I haven't," I said. "I'm so happy to be with you guys. It's made all the difference at Alta Mesa. Having you for friends gives me a little corner where I feel like I belong."

Roni finished doing my makeup and put a light coating of hair spray over my hair. "There. Perfect," she said. "Okay, let's get going. Time to meet Sean Baxter and destiny!"

I examined my new, highlighted face in the mirror. "Now all we have to do is pray that my mother doesn't notice I'm wearing makeup and make me wash it off."

But it seemed to be a night of miracles. My mother actually nodded approvingly when she saw me. "Very nice," she said. "Roni did your hair well. It suits you. And your father and I are glad that you accepted our decision about the camping trip without a fuss. Going to the symphony is a good way to spend an evening. You can't get in trouble at a concert."

I didn't look at Roni because I was sure I'd giggle or give myself away. If my mother only knew that my sole reason for going to the symphony was to meet a guy!

But Mom went on, not seeming to notice that Roni and I both had our lips pressed together, trying hard not to smile. "And your music teacher will be very pleased that you've taken the trouble to hear her play. She was telling me that you don't seem to be as enthusiastic about your music as you used to be."

I didn't dare open my mouth, so I just nodded.

"Have a good time," my mother said, smiling. "Are you sure it's only a short walk to your friend's house afterward? I don't want you walking around in the dark."

"It's very close, Mrs. Nguyen," Roni said, "and the streets are well lit. The concert should be over before ten. We'll be fine."

"Okay, then. Take care of each other," Mom said.

"We will," I muttered, and then we fled to my father's car before we laughed out loud.

We deliberately got to the concert early so that we could see where Sean was sitting. As we had guessed he was right in the front, next to an important-looking woman with frosted hair—obviously his mother, the symphony big wheel. She seemed to know everybody. She kept turning around to wave and talk to people. Sean sat very still in his seat and stared straight ahead of him. I got the feeling her behavior was embarrassing him, and my heart went out to him. He also suffered from bossy parents. How perfect!

There was no way we could talk to Sean before the concert started. Even if Roni wanted to, I wasn't going down to the front of the auditorium—not at the risk of confronting his terrifying mother. So we had to wait for the intermission. The first half of the program dragged on and on.

"Boy, classical music sure takes a long time," Roni whispered to me. "How many movements does a symphony have?"

"Four," I whispered.

"Seems like twenty-four," she whispered back, making me smile. It felt the same to me! In the seat next to me was a huge man who made snorting noises as he breathed. He was so large that his elbow stuck into me. In the seat next to Roni was a rich old lady who jangled her charm bracelets every time she moved. In the row behind us a man had fallen asleep and snored until his wife shook him awake.

"I hope you appreciate what I'm doing for you," Roni whispered.

"I hope Sean appreciates what I'm doing for him," I whispered back.

The symphony finally came to an end. The audience was still applauding as we stood up stiffly, slipped out of our row, and waited near the door Sean was likely to come through. I felt sure he'd found the first half of the concert as long as we had. He'd definitely need to leave his seat and stretch his legs.

It seemed like the whole auditorium had emptied before Sean finally came out. He was wearing a blazer and tie, and he looked very serious and grown-up. I shot Roni a worried look. "What do we do now?" I whispered.

"Leave it to me," she said. "Just play along . . . and don't giggle!"

She pushed through the crowd as if she were about to go back in through the door we had just come out of. She brushed against Sean, catching his attention. When he looked at her, she stopped and said, "Oh, hi. Don't you go to my school? Alta Mesa?"

Sean looked confused. "Yeah . . ."

"I've seen you at orchestra practice," Roni went on brightly.

"Oh, you're in the orchestra?" Sean asked. He looked even more confused now. "I don't think—"

"No, *I'm* not," Roni said quickly, "but I slip in sometimes to listen to my friend Karen." She grabbed my arm and thrust me forward. "You know Karen, don't you? First violin?"

Sean looked at me and smiled. "Oh, yeah. Karen. I've seen you. And heard you. You're pretty good."

"Thanks." I couldn't really say he was good, too, because I hadn't heard him play alone. But I had to say something. "Y-you play oboe, don't you?" I stammered.

He nodded. "The woodwinds sound pretty terrible."

"Not *that* bad," I said. "Some of the clarinets—"

"All of the clarinets," he said, "are hopeless."

We had exhausted that topic. We stood there, shifting uncomfortably from foot to foot.

"So what do you think of the orchestra conductor?" Sean asked at last.

"She's a little too explosive for me," I said. "She makes me jump when she yells."

"Yeah, she's very dramatic, but she's harmless," he said. "I think she does it to cover up that she's a lousy conductor."

"Really?"

"Well, she's not very good, is she?" Sean demanded. "I mean, have you played with the Phoenix Youth Orchestra?"

I shook my head.

"Now there's a conductor who knows what he's doing. Brahms's Second? No problem—and that's not the easiest piece to tackle with a bunch of kids."

I nodded.

"You should try out for the Youth Orchestra," he said. "It looks good on your résumé if you want to wind up in Juilliard or one of the big conservatories."

"Is that what you want to do?" I asked.

"Naturally. It's the only way to go. I can't understand these people who settle for Arizona State. It's a waste of time for serious musicians."

I nodded again. I was beginning to feel like one of those toy dogs that sit in a car window, my head going up and down as Sean talked.

"Who do you study with?" he asked after another pause.

"Mrs. Hetherton. Do you know her? She's playing with this orchestra. The violinist with the gray hair in a bun."

"Oh, her," Sean said. "Is she any good? She looks wimpy."

"She's been my teacher since I was five."

"Then maybe it's time to move on," he said. "I could ask my mother for suggestions. She knows every music teacher in this town. She's on the board of the music chest that hands out scholarships."

"I guess Mrs. Hetherton's okay," I said weakly.

"Well, let me know if you want to change. You're a freshman, aren't you? Only four years until you start on your serious training."

"*If* I want to be a musician," I snapped. I hadn't meant to say that—it just popped out.

Sean looked confused. "Why on earth are you studying if you don't want to take it up seriously?" he asked.

I wanted to say that my parents were the ones who dreamed of a musical future for me, but I didn't want to risk offending him. "I just meant that fourteen is very young to start thinking about my future."

"She wants to enjoy high school first," Roni chimed in. "Have fun, make friends . . . What do you do for fun, Sean?"

"I have so little time," he said. "What with music practice and homework."

"I know," I said. "It's the same for me."

"I suppose it will all be worth it someday."

"I suppose so," I agreed, although at the moment I doubted it. The lights flashed to signify the end of intermission.

"I'm sorry, we kept you from getting anything at the snack bar," Roni said to Sean. "We're going out for ice cream afterward. Want to join us?"

"Oh, no, thanks," he said. "We usually have people back to the house after these concerts. I have to be there to hand out food and help clean up."

"See you at school, then," Roni said.

"Uh . . . sure," he replied. His mother was approaching like a ship in full sail. Sean shot us a quick smile and headed back inside.

"So what do you think?" Roni whispered as we made our way back to our seats.

"I don't know what to think," I admitted. "He didn't swoon at the sight of me."

"We knew he was shy," Roni said. "It will take time. But you two hit it off pretty well. You had stuff to talk about."

"Sure," I said. "We lead very similar lives."

"There you are," Roni said. "I bet he'll be real friendly in orchestra on Monday. I bet he's kicking himself that he can't come out with us tonight."

I didn't answer. I was fighting with disappointment. Things hadn't gone the way I had dreamed they would. I had thought this concert would be a turning point in my life. And now it was half over, and nothing had changed at all.

Chapter 6

Justine looked surprised as she opened her front door. "You're early," she said, tying a terry-cloth robe over her bathing suit. "I didn't expect you before eleven. What happened? Wasn't he there?"

"He was there," Roni said.

"But you didn't get to meet him?"

"Sure we did. Everything went just the way we planned it. He and Karen talked about music and stuff and we invited him out afterward, but he had to go home. He was with his parents."

"What a geek," Justine said.

"You haven't seen his mother," Roni told her. "She didn't look like someone who takes no for an answer."

"So you two hit it off?" Justine asked me. "You

and Sean, I mean. Not you and his mother."

"We talked," I said. "That was a start, I suppose."

"That's all?" Justine asked. "Did his eyes light up when he saw you? Did your heart beat faster when you were close to him? Did you feel an electric tingle when his sleeve brushed against yours?"

"I don't really remember," I said.

"You don't remember? What kind of romantic encounter was that?"

"I was so nervous, Justine," I explained. "I was just concentrating on not saying something dumb."

"Well, did he ask to see you again?"

"He said he'd see me in school."

"That's a start," Justine said. "And do you want to see him again, Karen?"

"Sure . . . I guess," I said. "He seemed like a nice enough guy."

"You don't sound like you just met your soul mate," Justine said. "I wonder if that dork Walter really knows what he's doing with his computer matching. I mean, if he couldn't come up with a guy for me, then maybe he goofed on you and Sean."

"No way!" Roni said. "Sean is just right for her. I was watching them while they talked. He's exactly the right height, and he has a nice voice and big brown eyes and he's really into music. He couldn't be more perfect."

I didn't know what to say. Roni seemed so sure that Sean and I were made for each other. But privately, I was beginning to think Justine was right—maybe Walter's program really didn't work. If I had truly met my perfect guy, wouldn't I feel something magical?

Justine led us into a changing room, and Roni and I wriggled into our bathing suits. "Where's Ginger?" Roni asked.

"Oh, she's out in the hot tub," Justine said.

"She didn't wait for us?" Roni sounded surprised.

"She was acting kind of strange tonight," Justine said, lowering her voice. "Really remote, like she had something on her mind. But whenever I asked her about it, she just snapped at me. She said she wanted to be alone, so I let her go ahead."

"She's been acting strange for the last week or so," I said. "I thought I might be imagining it, but you and Roni have noticed it too. Something really must be wrong between her and Ben."

"Or at home?" Justine suggested. "People don't always like to talk about problems at home. I know I don't."

"But I'm always in her home," Roni said. "I could sense if something wasn't right. And she'd tell me, too. She's always told me everything."

"Maybe she just doesn't feel good," Justine said,

pushing open the door that led to the back patio. "I'm always a grouch when I've got a cold coming on."

"Maybe that's it," Roni agreed. "And there are a lot of allergies this time of year. That could explain it."

"I think we should try to find out what's wrong so we can help her," I said.

"But I know Ginger. She won't tell us if she doesn't want to," Roni argued.

"Then we'll have to worm it out of her subtly," Justine said. "We'll just drop little hints. She won't even realize that she's telling us."

Roni looked at me and giggled. "When have you ever been subtle, Justine?" she asked. "Your idea of worming it out of her is probably throwing her against the wall and saying, 'Okay Ginger. Tell us what's wrong or else!'"

"I can be subtle if I want to," Justine said. "You just watch me."

We headed out to the patio. Justine's pool sparkled with clear blue light and the little lights around the patio threw a green glow on the shrubs and palm trees, turning her backyard into a fairyland. At one end of the pool there was a separate hot tub. Ginger sat in it surrounded by steam, staring out into the darkness.

"Hi, Ginger, how's the water?" Roni yelled.

Ginger continued to stare up at the stars, "Fine," she said.

"You could have waited for us," Roni said, sitting on the stone bench to take off her shoes.

"I thought you might not show up," Ginger replied.

"What? You knew we were coming," Roni said.

"I thought you might be hanging out with Sean and his friends until it was really late," she said. "Or Karen might have gone off somewhere with Sean. Or you might have gone home."

"What are you talking about?" Roni demanded.

"Well, you might have been too tired to bother coming here," Ginger said.

Roni stared at Ginger as though she'd lost her mind. "Ginger, we said we'd come. When have I ever not shown up when I said I would?"

"I don't know," Ginger said. "Things change, don't they? People change."

"What's with you, anyway?" Roni demanded.

"Nothing. I'm fine," Ginger snapped.

Roni perched on the edge of the hot tub. "Look, if something's wrong . . ."

"I said I'm fine. Don't bug me," Ginger growled.

"Okay. Okay," Roni said, backing away.

"So how was your concert?" Ginger asked.

"Boring," Roni said. "If that's classical music, give me rock any day. Each of the pieces lasted about five hours."

81

"Roni, the whole concert was only two and a half hours," I said.

"It felt like five hours," Roni replied. "Especially with that guy snoring down my neck."

I started laughing. "You do exaggerate."

"He was," Roni said, laughing with me. "Every time he fell asleep, he leaned forward and started snoring into my neck."

"Well, I had it worse," I told her. "That fat old guy in the seat next to me had his elbow stuck into my side. I had to hold my breath all night!"

"But it was worth it," Roni said. "We met Sean and you talked to him."

"Was it love at first sight?" Ginger asked.

"I'm not sure," I said. "I think love at first sight only happens in books. If he's as shy as I am, it will take a while to get to know each other. He's probably not very comfortable around girls, and I certainly don't have a clue how to act around boys."

"You two seemed really comfortable," Roni protested. "Once you got onto music, there was no problem."

I climbed into the hot tub. The warm bubbles tingled, and I sank onto the seat with a contented sigh. "I've been looking forward to this," I said.

"Yeah, it's great," Roni agreed, coming to sit beside me. "Don't the stars look bright tonight?"

"Fantastic," I agreed. "Close enough to touch."

"I bet they look even better up at the lake," Justine said.

"Did you have to remind us?" Roni wailed. "All through that dreary concert I kept telling myself that I could have been with Drew, sitting by a campfire and watching the moonlight on the water."

"And I'm sure you'd rather be watching the moonlight with Ben, Ginger," Justine said, giving Roni and me a knowing look.

"Sure, but—" Ginger began.

"It must bug you that he likes to spend Saturday night with his buddies instead of with you," Justine interrupted. "I mean, you don't even know whether you're his real girlfriend. He's never actually come out and asked you to go steady with him, has he?"

"No, but he doesn't have to," Ginger said. "I know how he's feeling."

"But it must bother you that he's always somewhere else and you're stuck with us girls."

"No," Ginger said, frowning. "He's been getting together with the same guys every Saturday for years. I wouldn't want to spoil that for him."

"Then I guess you're glad to get away from home for the night," Justine continued. "I mean, I know if I have problems at home, I can't wait to get away—"

"What is this?" Ginger asked, rising to her feet.

83

"Are you trying to be a psychologist, Justine?"

"Me? A psychologist?" Justine said with a fake laugh.

"I'm not totally stupid," Ginger said. "What's with all the questions about my problems with Ben and at home?"

"I confess. I *am* getting interested in psychology," Justine said.

"Then why are you only bugging me?" Ginger demanded. "Why don't you bug Roni or Karen instead? They both have as many hang-ups as I do."

"It was just that I thought . . . we thought that . . ."

"What?"

"Nothing, really."

"Then get off my case," Ginger said. "You guys are acting really weird." She climbed out of the hot tub and wrapped her towel around herself. "I'm getting too hot. I think I'll go change."

We watched her go.

"Way to be subtle, Justine," Roni said.

"I was just trying to help," Justine said in a hurt voice.

"Sure you were," I said gently. "I guess Ginger has problems she doesn't want to share right now. Maybe we should leave her alone."

"Yeah, maybe we should be devoting all our energy to turning Karen and Sean into the romance of

84

the century," Justine said. "How can we arrange a really romantic meeting for them at school?"

"Lock them in the music closet together?" Roni suggested.

"You guys can't arrange anything," I said. "If something's going to happen between Sean and me, it just has to happen by itself. If he feels he's being trapped into meeting me, then I'm sure he'll run in the other direction as fast as he can."

"But he's shy, Karen. He might have to be prodded a little," Roni said. "This needs some careful thought."

She lay back, watching the stars. I did the same. The sky was like black velvet and the stars were spread across it like diamonds, twinkling and shining. I felt my disappointment returning. I knew I had been expecting too much from tonight. I'd built it up in my mind, dreaming about how our eyes would meet, how we would immediately connect. I thought when I met Sean it would be as if nobody else existed in the whole world. But it hadn't been like that at all. Sean's eyes hadn't lit up when he saw me. And I couldn't help realizing that mine hadn't lit up either—not the way they would have if he'd been the guy of my dreams.

Chapter

7

On Monday morning I had planned to meet Roni at my locker. I was just getting out my books for first period when I felt something brush against my leg. I spun around just in time to see that familiar cape flying out as Weird Waldo ran down the hall. He didn't seem to notice that his cape was touching people on either side of him, or that he was getting some pretty strange looks as he went past. What was with that guy, anyway? I simply couldn't understand why someone would act so antisocial.

I was so intent on watching Waldo that I jumped when I felt a tap on my shoulder. "Relax, it's only me, not Sean," Roni said, grinning at my terrified expression. "I spent all yesterday trying to come up with the perfect way to get you and Sean together. Don't forget, if he's really shy, you have to make the first move. Maybe there's another concert coming up that you can ask him to?"

"I don't know, Roni," I said. "I'm no good at talking to boys."

"I guess I could find an excuse to come into orchestra and help you out," she suggested.

"No," I said firmly. "I have to do this myself. If it's meant to be, then it will happen."

"Okay," Roni said. "I wonder how the weekend at the lake went. I haven't seen Drew yet."

As if on cue, the double doors at the end of the hall burst open and a noisy group of kids came in. Before I'd even had a chance to turn around I heard Drew's voice yelling, "Hey, Roni!" down the hall.

He ran toward her with long, easy strides and put his hand on her shoulder. "Hey, how's it going?" he asked. His eyes were smiling into hers. Her whole face was glowing as she looked at him. I felt a surge of envy. Not only did she have a cute guy standing with his hand on her shoulder, but she seemed completely relaxed around him. I couldn't understand how she did it.

"How was the lake?" Roni asked. "I was so mad my folks wouldn't let me go."

"You didn't miss much," Drew said, making a face. "It turned into a total bummer."

"What happened?"

"We got busted. The cops came."

"Why?"

"It started off with an illegal campfire. Then they found out there wasn't an adult present and some of the older kids had beer, so they called my folks and we got sent home."

"Oh, Drew. That *is* a bummer."

"Yeah, it was pretty embarrassing," he said. "I hate being treated like a little kid. I guess they shouldn't have had beer, though."

"That's true," Roni said.

"Oh, well. There will be other weekends, other parties," he said. "And now I know not to hang out with some of those kids." He ruffled her hair. "Gotta run. See ya!" He moved to catch up with his friends.

"Can you imagine that?" Roni asked me as we moved down the hall to where Ginger and Justine were waiting for us.

"I was just trying to picture what my folks would have said if I'd been to a camp-out that got busted by the police," I said. "They'd probably lock me up until I was forty."

"Mine wouldn't have been too pleased, either," Roni said. "Maybe parents do know what they're talking about."

"Sometimes!" I said.

At that moment Charlene Davies stepped out of the girls' room right in front of us. She was looking more perfect than ever, her blond hair pulled back in a ponytail, wearing a lacy top and little red shorts. As usual, she was surrounded by a bunch of other cheerleaders.

"So how was the lake, Charlene?" one of them asked.

"Fantastic. See my tan?"

Then she pretended to notice Roni for the first time. "Oh, hi, Roni," she purred. "Too bad you couldn't come up to the lake with us. I heard your parents wouldn't let you."

"I thought you hated bugs," Roni said.

"Whatever gave you that idea?" Charlene asked sweetly. "I wouldn't have missed it for the world. It was such fun."

"That's not what Drew told me," Roni said. "I heard the police made you leave."

"Not until almost morning. We had lots of fun first." She gave a little giggle and disappeared down the hall.

Roni was glaring after her. "Drew said she wasn't going," she muttered. "I wonder what made her change her mind?"

"Don't worry about it. Drew looked happy to see you just now," I said. "She's only trying to make you jealous."

"Well," Roni said, "I'm not worried about her. Drew's forgotten she even exists."

She stalked into our classroom and slammed her books down on the desk. I gave Ginger a worried glance, but Ginger just shrugged. For the rest of the period Roni scribbled furiously in her notebook. She didn't look in my direction once, even when the teacher said something funny.

But I had too much on my mind to worry about Roni for long. Orchestra was my last class before lunch. My stomach felt as if it were twisted into a tight knot at the thought of seeing Sean again. Would this be the moment when things would click between us? Would his face light up when he saw me come into the room? I hoped so, but I kept telling myself not to hope for too much. Being let down really hurt—I had learned that much from Saturday night.

The morning dragged on and on. At last I grabbed my violin from the music storeroom and stepped into the orchestra chamber. Some kids were already there, tuning up. I went to my seat and busied myself with my violin, trying not to look around for Sean. I had decided to let him come over to me if he was interested. I was just rubbing resin on my bow when he showed up.

"Hi, Karen," he said.

"Hi, Sean."

We smiled at each other. I remembered what Roni had said about making the first move.

"So . . . uh . . . did you recover from Saturday's concert yet?" I asked.

"Recover?" He looked confused.

"I meant from sitting through all those long pieces."

"Oh. I thought it was pretty good. One of the better performances of Sibelius, didn't you think?"

He'd actually liked it. I had no idea what to say.

"I'm not really familiar with Sibelius," I told him.

"I find him a very haunting composer," Sean said. "You should get acquainted with his work. In fact, they're playing a Sibelius overture on public TV on Thursday."

"They are?"

He nodded. "Why don't you listen to it? I'd be interested to get your reaction. I could call you afterward and we could talk about it. What's your phone number?"

He was asking for my phone number! I told him, and he wrote it down neatly in his little notebook.

"This is great," he said. "There aren't too many people in this school who enjoy discussing music—real music, I mean, not that horrible rock noise. I keep hoping those rock singers will explode with their amplifiers, but they never do!"

He was grinning as if he'd just made a big joke. I couldn't believe I'd ever thought I had anything in common with him—he sounded like my father! "Don't you think that would be satisfying," he continued, "watching a heavy-metal band launched into space, still playing their instruments? Come to think of it, that might make a better sound than they usually produce!"

I was doing my best to smile politely. "You know, Karen," Sean said hesitantly. "You could come over to my place on Thursday. We can watch the TV concert together! I'm sure it would be okay with my mom. She's always telling me to make friends who are interested in music."

I was really tempted to tell him that I already had tickets to a hard-rock concert for Thursday, but my super-polite upbringing wouldn't let me do that. Instead I mumbled, "I'm afraid my parents don't let me go out on school nights. I have to get in my three hours of violin practice."

"Oh, I understand totally," he said, nodding. "Some other time, then."

"Sure," I said. I didn't even watch him as he headed back to his seat.

At the end of orchestra I put away my violin and was one of the first people out of the room. I arrived at our tree to find my friends sitting with the nerds.

"So, Karen, we're dying to hear. How did your dream date go?" Owen asked.

"What happened in orchestra? Did he come talk to you?" Roni practically shouted.

All those faces were staring at me so expectantly, I almost told them what they wanted to hear: "Yes, he spoke to me and we're getting together to listen to music at his place." But I found myself shaking my head. "He did talk to me," I said.

"And?" Justine yelled.

"And he asked for my phone number . . ."

"Way to go, Karen!" Owen and Walter gave each other high fives, as if they were personally responsible for this triumph.

"And he invited me over to his place on Thursday to listen to a concert on public TV."

"Karen, that's perfect," Roni said excitedly. "It couldn't have worked out better. I'm so happy for you."

"I haven't finished yet," I said.

"He asked you to fly to Europe with him for a Mozart festival?" Roni quipped.

"I told him I was busy on Thursday," I finished.

Now all those eyes were looking at me in amazed horror.

"Karen! Why did you say that?"

"I just didn't want to go."

"You what?"

"I'm sorry," I said, looking from one face to the next, "but Sean is just not the guy for me. He's boring. He's narrow-minded and he's opinionated. I like music, that's true, but that doesn't mean I have to live, breathe, and talk music all the time. Life is more than boring old symphonies."

They were all stunned.

"But, Karen, we were so sure," Justine said at last.

"He seemed so perfect," Roni added.

"The computer can't be wrong," Walter said firmly. "It gave you a ninety percent compatibility rating."

"I said I was sorry. What more can I say?" I looked around the circle. "Look, I really tried. I didn't feel anything for him on Saturday, but I put that down to nerves. But today he was actually beginning to annoy me, and that's only the second conversation we've ever had."

"See, Walter, I told you your dumb computer program didn't work," Justine said. "It couldn't come up with a match for me, and it came up with the wrong one for Karen."

"There's nothing wrong with my program," Walter said. "It's not my fault if you feed it stupid information. If you give it the correct data, it will be one hundred percent accurate, one hundred percent of the time. Come down to the computer lab and I'll prove it to you."

"How can you prove it?" Ginger asked.

"Simple," Walter said, herding us down the path like a dog with a flock of sheep. "We'll select a couple we know are completely compatible and we'll get the computer to run their compatibility rating. You'll see. A machine can't be wrong."

We reached the computer lab and went inside. It was empty. Apparently the nerds were the only people who used the computers outside of class. Walter sat down at a computer.

"Okay," he said, looking around at the rest of us. "Give me a couple."

"Wouldn't it make more sense to find Karen a new guy?" Justine demanded.

"I have to prove to you that my program works," Walter said. "What couple do we know who are completely right for each other?"

"Me and Drew," Roni said quickly.

"Fair enough, Roni and Drew," Walter said. "I have all the information on Drew already in my database. Now I need information on you."

Roni patiently answered the questions on her hobbies and interests, her likes and dislikes. Then Walter asked the machine to compute. It seemed to take a long time. Finally the message came up on the screen: COMPATIBILITY FACTOR: 2.

"Two?" Roni asked. "What's that supposed to mean? Is two good or bad?"

Walter's face had gone beet red. "Compatibility is rated on a scale of one to ten," he said.

"Meaning what?" Roni's eyes were flashing now.

"Meaning that ten is a perfect match."

"And two?"

"And two has very little in common. Not much chance of making it as a couple."

"You're saying that Drew and I have nothing in common?" Roni yelled. "See? I knew it was too good to be true! He lied to me last weekend. He knew Charlene was going and he said she wasn't. He still likes her better after all. I bet she and he come out as a ten."

"I could run that for you if you're really—" Walter began.

"Oh, shut up!" Roni cut him off. "Just forget the whole thing. I was stupid to believe that a guy like Drew would be interested in a nobody like me!" She pushed past us and ran out the door.

"Thanks a lot, Walter. You've screwed up just about everybody's life with your stupid program," Ginger said angrily. "Come on, let's get out of here before he tells me that Ben and I secretly hate each other's guts."

She headed for the door. Justine was right behind her, but I hung back. I felt bad for Walter and his friends. After all, they had genuinely tried to help us. It wasn't their fault that Sean and I hadn't clicked or that Roni and Drew were hopelessly incompatible.

"I'm sorry, guys," I said. "I know you meant well."

"The program does work, honestly," Walter said. "It has to work. Why don't you let us try you again, Karen? I'm sure we could come up with another guy for you."

"Thanks, but—"

"Oh, come on, give Walter another chance," Owen said. "You've really bruised his ego today. He prides himself on his computer programs."

"Well, okay, I guess," I said, "but not today. I should go with my friends. Roni's pretty upset. You know how she feels about Drew."

"Maybe tomorrow, then?" Walter suggested. "I'm not sure whether I can make it during tomorrow's lunch period, but I'll try. Meet me here. And you don't have to tell the others. They're all mad at me."

"Okay, I'll come alone," I said.

"Next time I guarantee the boy of your dreams," Walter promised. "My database can't goof up twice in a row!"

Chapter

8

I almost didn't go to the computer lab the next day. In my heart, I really didn't believe that Walter was going to match me up with the guy of my dreams. I don't think I even believed that the guy of my dreams existed—and if he did, then a nerd like Walter probably wouldn't know how to match me with him. Besides, even if Walter did by chance make a match, my parents wouldn't let me go out with him until I turned sixteen. It was hopeless.

But that morning, something happened to make me change my mind. I had been noticing a strange tension among my friends for the past week. Ginger was acting weird. One minute she ignored us and didn't take part in our conversation, the next she snapped at everything we said. Roni, Justine, and I still had no idea why she was acting this way. We tried to behave as though nothing was going on, but it was starting to get on everyone's nerves.

And after Roni found out that she and Drew weren't compatible, all she could talk about was how miserable she was and how rotten her life was. Between the two of them, Justine and I were afraid to even breathe. When Roni and Ginger are both upset at the same time, you have the makings of a really big fight.

Roni can't do anything quietly—she has to be dramatic about getting a splinter in her finger! All morning I watched her in class. She sat there, staring straight ahead of her, almost as if she were actually paying attention to the teacher. But every now and then she gave a big sigh. Then she doodled RONI AND DREW with a heart around it on her binder. And then she scribbled it out with bold, black ink.

On the way to our tree for lunch, she worried out loud. "I should have known," she said. "It was too good to be true! I mean, you can't throw chili all over someone and expect them to fall in love with you, can you?"

"It's okay, Roni," I told her, patting her arm. "I'm sure you've got nothing to worry about."

"Thanks, Karen, but I can't help it," Roni said. "I

just have this awful feeling that my relationship with Drew is doomed. My whole life is doomed. I'm doomed."

"Roni, give it a break," Ginger snapped.

Roni looked as if Ginger had hit her. "Give it a break? You don't think it's important?"

"I think you're making a big deal about nothing," Ginger said. "It's a dumb computer program invented by a creepy nerd. Why should you believe it? It didn't work for Karen or Justine—why should it be right for you?"

"Because I sensed it all along, that's why," Roni said. "I kept telling myself things were too good to last. Drew and I aren't really alike. He's popular and I'm a nobody. All we had in common was a few accidents. I bet he knew all along that I wouldn't be able to go to the lake and that Charlene was going. I'll never find another guy like him. I'll probably never fall in love for the rest of my life!"

"For pete's sake, chill out," Ginger said.

"You should care that I'm feeling down," Roni said in a hurt voice. "You're supposed to be my best friend."

"Well, you could have fooled me," Ginger said.

"What's that supposed to mean?"

"You know very well."

"No, I don't, or I wouldn't say it."

"Then I'm not going to tell you."

"You're being totally childish!" Roni yelled. "You've been acting weird all week. Now you're being childish *and* weird."

"Me being childish? I like that!" Ginger yelled back. "I'm not the person who's having a fit because a computer program says she isn't compatible with her boyfriend."

"Fine, then don't support me in my hour of need," Roni said.

"I'm sure Karen will be happy to listen to your trauma," Ginger said.

Me? What did I have to do with this? I looked from Roni to Ginger. Ginger was glaring at both of us. There was a moment of complete silence. Then Justine glanced at me and shrugged. "I think I'll go finish up my math homework in the library," she said.

"And I promised Walter I'd let him reprogram me," I replied, following her away from Ginger and Roni as fast as I could.

Justine grinned. "Reprogram you as what, that's the question," she said. "I wouldn't be surprised if you came back as a three-headed mushroom from outer space."

"You mean one of Walter's close relatives?" I asked.

*   *   *

When I first went into the computer lab, the blinds were drawn and I didn't think anybody was there. Nerds always moved in packs, I knew. Walter was never without Owen, Wolfgang, and Ronald. I didn't know whether to wait or head back to our tree. But then I saw a movement at the far end of the room. Someone was working at one of the computers in the back row.

"So you managed to get here," I called brightly. "Have you found a dream date for me?"

The boy at the computer scrambled to his feet, and I saw that it wasn't Walter at all. It was Weird Waldo. He was still wearing the black cape and broad-brimmed hat. With his cape swirling around him, he reminded me of Batman. But his face was positively unheroic as he jumped up from his seat.

"I'm sorry," he muttered. "I didn't think anyone . . . I mean, the lab's usually free at lunchtime . . ."

His eyes darted around the room, as though he were planning his escape route.

"It's okay," I said uneasily, "I can come back some other time."

While I was speaking, I couldn't help wondering why they called him Weird Waldo and whether he was dangerous. The room was suddenly very dark, and the door seemed a long way behind me.

"No, I'll get out for you," he said quickly. "I just

wanted to try this idea . . . but it's okay. I can do it some other time."

"You don't have to leave," I said. "You were here first."

"But . . . " he began, looking from his computer screen to my face as if thinking this over.

"You got here first," I repeated. "Besides, we were just fooling around in here. It wasn't a class or anything."

"Well, I'm just fooling around, too," he said. "I got this idea this morning in math and it wouldn't go away, so I had to try it out."

"What sort of idea?"

"A pretty dumb one, really," he said.

I took a step toward his computer. I could see that he was considering switching it off to wipe out his idea before I saw it. But he didn't.

"I do computer graphics," he said, holding out his hands as if he were apologizing.

I looked at the screen. There was a cube on it, made up of lots of little cubes, and it was slowly rotating. As it rotated, all the lines of little cubes rotated, too. The figure was completely three-dimensional, suspended against a blue background. I almost felt as if it would twirl right out of the screen.

"That's absolutely incredible," I said, leaning closer for a better look. "How did you do it?"

"It took a while," he said, "and it's kind of compli-cated to explain. I've been using this graphics pro-gram that lets you see things from different perspectives. I put in a command to keep the figure rotating until I tell it to stop."

"Wow," I said. "I've never seen anything like this before."

I pulled up a chair and sat down.

"It's pretty basic as far as computer graphics go," Weird Waldo said.

"Basic?" I said. "It's amazing! The most I can do with a computer is put in someone else's program and press enter. You actually thought this up?"

He nodded. "I've got this crazy idea. I'm trying to create a three-dimensional animal and make it move, as if it's walking out of the screen."

"Wow, that sounds incredibly cool," I said.

"I've got a long way to go yet," he said, "but I've seen it done at computer graphics exhibitions. You have to create the figure in various poses and then tell the computer to make it move logically between the poses. That's how they re-create dinosaurs on screen."

"Is there anything else you can show me?" I asked. "Any other figures you can do right now?"

Weird Waldo shook his head. "I've got a lot of stuff at home, but I don't have my disks here with me," he said. "I've done one pretty neat thing that's like a solar system. The planets rotate among themselves and around a central sun."

"I'd love to see that," I blurted without thinking.

I saw his face go pink. "Well, I . . ." he stammered.

I turned red, too. "Look, I wasn't inviting myself over or anything. I'm sorry. I guess I just got carried away—this is all so new to me."

"You really like it, don't you?" he asked quietly.

"I really like it."

"So . . ." He cleared his throat. "You're into computers?"

"Me?" I laughed. "I told you, I know nothing about computers. And I wasn't even interested before this. I mean, databases and stuff are Walter's thing, not mine. I don't even like video games. I always get killed by the monster right away."

"Me too," he said. "That's why I'm working on one in which nothing eats you or kills you. It's a three-dimensional maze and you have to find your way out, only the maze keeps rearranging itself."

"Sounds like one of my nightmares," I said, shuddering.

"One of mine, too, actually," Weird Waldo said, looking at me with interest. "That's why I started it. I thought if I could conquer it on the screen, I wouldn't dream about it at night."

"In my dream I always think I've found the way

out, but I've misjudged the size," I said. "When I get to the exit, I'm way too big to get through. Like Alice in Wonderland."

"Me too," he said, "And you try crawling through, but your head hits the ceiling."

"Yes!" I yelled.

We looked at each other and laughed.

"Then I guess you're as mixed up as I am," he said.

"I don't think you're mixed up," I said. "I think you're very creative."

"I don't think like most other people do," he said. "I have these ideas that are really off the wall. They seem normal and possible to me, but everyone else is always looking at me as if I'm crazy, or else they're laughing at me."

"But that's what all really creative people have to go through," I said. "A lot of people are scared of anything that they can't understand. They laugh to cover their nervousness."

Weird Waldo pulled up a chair and sat on it backward, straddling the seat with his arms resting on the back. "Are you creative, too?"

"No, I'm just ordinary," I said with a smile. "At least, I think I am. I haven't had much opportunity to try anything creative. I've been playing the violin since I was five. All those hours of practice sure eat up the day."

"Oh, so you're a musician. That's creative."

"Only because that's what I've been forced into," I said. "I really don't know what I feel about music. I mean, I like it. I like playing my violin in the orchestra, but I can't help feeling that there's more to life than three hours of practice every night. It just doesn't feel very creative to me, because I have no choice about whether to do it or not."

"Three hours of practice. That's pretty heavy," he said. "Are your parents musicians?"

"No. They came from Vietnam before I was born. Their own childhood got messed up by the war. But they both like music, and they wanted me to do something special with my life."

"I agree with that," he said. "Everyone should do something special with their lives."

"Only, I don't think I want it to be music."

"Then what?"

"I don't know. I don't think that I could ever do what you're doing with computers. I don't think I'm very artistic, but that doesn't stop me from enjoying art. Maybe I'm just designed to be a spectator."

"Don't say that," he said. "You shouldn't settle for watching anyone else's life. You have to find what you want to do and then put everything you've got into it. Most people don't do that. They just exist. They don't even know they're alive."

"You're right," I said. "Is that why you chose to do independent study instead of regular classes?"

"How did you know that?"

"Owen and his friends told me. They said you did your own thing in school."

"I do, pretty much. Regular classes bore me. And I don't enjoy being laughed at, either."

"Then why do you dress like—" I began, but I quickly shut myself up.

"Why do I dress like this?" he finished for me. "To show people they can't hurt me, I guess."

"But . . . excuse me for saying this . . ." I went on hesitantly, "wouldn't they tease you less if you dressed like other people?"

He smiled. "This all started a long time ago," he said. "In first grade everyone decided I was different. Well, I was. My parents are both college professors. They had always treated me as if I were a little adult. You can imagine how the other kids looked at me when I said 'We should all learn to communicate verbally' every time some kid wanted to punch me!"

I had to laugh.

"When we did math, I could multiply in my head while everyone else was learning to carry tens," he went on. "I knew about fractions and decimals. I thought I was being helpful when I showed the other kids short cuts in their work. I wanted them to like me. But they thought I was showing off. It was hopeless. And my mother never made it easier for me. She dressed me in her version of sensible school clothes—white shirts and bow ties and stuff like that. After a while I decided that if people wanted to laugh at me, fine. So I started dressing as differently as possible. I just wanted them to leave me alone."

"And is that what you still want . . . uh . . . Waldo? Is that your name?"

"Weird Waldo is just what everyone calls me," he said. "My name is James. That's a pretty wimpy name, too, come to think of it. You never hear of a football player called James."

"Charles Barclay is one of the best basketball players around and Charles is a wimpy name," I said.

He nodded. "Yeah, he's awesome, isn't he? I'd love to play like him."

"Do you play basketball?"

"I tried out once," he said, "but I didn't get along too well with the coach. I explained to him that the drills he was giving us were actually stretching the opposite muscles from the ones we needed for jumping skills. He told me to shut up and sit down. I never went back."

I laughed.

"What about you? Are you into sports?"

"Only watching."

"You like the Suns?"

"You bet. I always watch on TV. I never went to a real game, though. My parents aren't exactly sports fans."

"Mine either," James said. "I have to sneak into my room to watch basketball."

"I don't have a TV in my room. I have to flip back quickly to opera if my folks come in."

"Your house sounds almost as wacky as mine," he said.

"You better believe it," I told him. "By the way, I'm Karen."

"Karen. That's a nice name. It suits you."

"James suits you, too. I like James. It's sort of dignified and dependable."

"I'm not very dignified," he said, "but I'm pretty dependable—to my friends, that is. If I say something, I mean it. And I mean it when I say that—"

A loud ringing sound above our heads made us both jump. Then we realized it was the bell.

"Lunch can't be over already," I said. "It just started."

But the clock on the wall said one-fifteen. We looked at each other in amazement.

"I'm sorry," James said. "You didn't get to eat."

"I'll survive."

"You won't die of starvation before the end of school?"

111

"I'll grab a carrot stick on my way to Spanish," I said.

He rummaged in his backpack. "Here, take this," he said.

"What is it?"

"It's a power bar—high protein, high energy. It will keep you going better than a carrot stick." He held it out to me.

"But what about you?" I asked. "I don't want you to be hungry because of me."

"I'll manage," he said. "I had a big breakfast this morning."

"No, I can't—"

"Take it," he said. He took my hand and curled my fingers around the bar. Suddenly I realized that our hands were clasped together. We both looked up, surprised.

"We'd better get to class," I said, a little shakily.

"Yeah."

Reluctantly he let go of my hand. I picked up my bag and headed for the door. "Thanks for the power bar, James," I said, turning back.

"My pleasure," he said, and he smiled at me. I noticed for the first time that he had the most wonderful smile. It seemed to start in his eyes and light up his whole face so he was sort of glowing. As I smiled back, something inside me started glowing, too.

Chapter

9

The rest of the day passed in a daze. I couldn't believe what had just happened: I had met a boy and we had chatted as if we'd known each other all our lives. For the first time ever, I hadn't rehearsed every word in my head to make sure it came out right. In fact, when I thought back to it, I couldn't actually remember the words we had used at all. It was as if we didn't need words to communicate.

When I went to my locker to get out my homework books, I found an interesting paper dart resting on my algebra book. It looked like a cross between a rocket ship and a pterodactyl, and I could see writing on the inside. Someone must have shoved it through the slats in my locker door. I glanced around before I opened it.

It was a short note, written in spiky slanted letters with a green pen:

I've been thinking about you all afternoon. You are the first person I have ever really talked to without feeling that I was being judged or laughed at. I can't wait to see you again.
                                                    James

"Hey, Karen," Justine's voice interrupted me. "Are you walking home? You want to go by the yogurt shop?"

"Uh . . . sorry, what did you say?" I asked, trying to focus on her face.

"Are you okay?" she asked.

"Fine. I'm fine."

"That's what Ginger keeps on saying, but she's definitely cracking up," Justine said. "I hope you're not going to be the next one to crack. You've got a funny look on your face—like you're spaced out."

"Oh, no," I said. "I'm really fine."

"What's that?" she asked, flicking James's note, which now hung limp in my hands.

Hurriedly I crumpled it up and tossed it into my backpack. "Uh . . . nothing. Just a note some kid wrote me in class."

"Come on, then. Let's go," she said. "I've got a ton of homework."

"Maybe we should skip the yogurt shop?" I suggested.

"Are you crazy? If anything gets skipped, it's the homework," she said, smiling as she pushed me ahead of her down the hall.

Later, on the way to my house, I wondered why I hadn't told Justine about James. She was one of my best friends. She'd probably be glad that I'd found a boy I could talk to, a boy I really wanted to be friends with. And yet I wasn't one hundred percent sure about that. Even the nerds had thought it was okay to make fun of James. I could just imagine what Justine might say. And I didn't want anybody saying anything mean about him.

The next morning when I got to school, I looked for James by my locker. I had been so sure he'd be waiting for me there that I felt a big rush of disappointment when there was no sign of him. I even looked up and down the hall a few times before I had to accept that he wasn't coming. With a sigh, I opened my locker to get out my books. A perfect red rose fell out.

Hurriedly I bent to pick it up, before any of my friends could notice. I was definitely intrigued. How did a rose get into my locker? I knew a paper dart could have been pushed through the slats—but a rose, round, red, and undamaged? There was no way.

It was really exciting to think that some guy had managed the impossible for me. I wanted to put the rose in water right away, so that it would stay alive a long, long time. But that was impossible in school. So I did the next-best thing. I pressed it between the pages of my algebra book. That way, I'd have it forever.

At lunchtime I lingered by my locker again, but there was no sign of James. I went to join my friends under our tree. There was a sort of unhappy truce between Roni and Ginger. They were trying to act normally, but most of their talking was done to me or Justine, not to each other.

"Did you talk to Drew yet?" Justine asked Roni.

Roni sighed. "You know what it's like during the week. He has student council meetings and football practice. He's never free for a moment." She took a savage bite of her peach. "Besides," she said when she had swallowed, "I don't want him to think I'm chasing him. I mean, if it's over, it's over. I'll just have to face it."

"Roni, Drew hasn't given you any sign that he doesn't want you around," I said. "I saw him the other morning. He ruffled your hair in the hallway and gave you a wonderful smile. Why should that have changed?"

"Because he's begun to realize how little we have in common," Roni said.

"I wish you would talk to him and sort this whole

dumb thing out," Justine said. "And I wish someone would shoot Walter. This is all his fault. It's making you depressed for nothing!"

"I hope it is for nothing," Roni said. "And I hope Walter really is off base with his program." She turned to me. "Sorry I didn't come to the lab yesterday. Did you find the guy of your dreams?"

"I . . . uh, that is . . ." I stammered. She had caught me completely off guard. How could she possibly know about James?

"Did Walter manage to come up with someone new for you?" Roni continued.

"Walter didn't show up," I said, relieved. I had forgotten all about Walter and his database.

"Too bad. I wonder if we could go find him today and make him keep his promise to you."

"It's okay," I said hastily. "I really don't want to go through that again."

"It was pretty embarrassing," Justine agreed. "But Karen, you do need a little help finding a guy you can get along with."

"Justine, you make it sound like she's totally hopeless," Roni said. "Karen's pretty and she's funny and she's nice. Once any guy gets to know her, he'll like her right away."

"But he'll never get to know her if she's so shy," Justine protested. "She'd never be able to talk to a guy on her own. I'm really bummed that Sean Baxter didn't work out. He still seems like the perfect date to me. Can't you give him another try, Karen? Maybe once your shyness wears off and his shyness wears off, you'd like each other."

She looked at me, expecting an answer, but I hadn't really been paying attention to what she was saying. Someone had come out of the art building, at the end of the path, and was standing in the shade, looking in my direction. Even at a distance I couldn't mistake the flowing cape. James just stood there, half hidden behind a pillar, watching me.

"Karen?" Justine repeated.

"Uh . . . sorry, I wasn't listening," I said. The cape flared as James turned and started walking away. I jumped to my feet. "I'll be right back," I told my friends. "There's someone I have to see."

I ran down the path and caught up with James just as he was about to go into the building again. I tapped his arm and he jumped.

"Hi," I said.

"Hi."

"I thought you were going to come over and talk to me."

"You were with people," he said. "I didn't want to embarrass you."

"Don't be silly. Why would you embarrass me?"

"Most girls would rather die than be seen with me."

"I'm not most girls."

"You're certainly not," he said, looking at me with deep brown eyes that made me feel warm inside.

"Thank you for the rose," I said. "At least, I guess it must have been from you—although I have no idea how you got it into my locker without squishing it."

He smiled. "My secret," he said. "Although it's no secret at all, really. Do you know how easy it is to open combination locks? You can actually hear the clicks. It's child's play."

"You mean I'm talking to a criminal?"

"I could be, if I wanted," he said. "But I'm usually not interested in breaking and entering."

"I'm glad you did this morning. Nobody's ever given me a flower before."

"I wanted to give it to you in person, but I chickened out," he said. "I didn't think you'd want to be seen with me."

"Will you stop putting yourself down?" I said. "You have to be one of the smartest guys in the school. You're good looking, you're thoughtful, and you're easy to talk to. You just happen to dress differently, that's all. People should be able to express their individuality. It's a free country."

He smiled. "It's funny to hear you say that. You're about the most conservative dresser in the school."

"That's because my mother chooses my clothes, not me," I said. "If I was given the choice, I'd wear jeans like everyone else."

"People should be able to express their individuality. Isn't that what you just said? It's a free country. Do you have any money of your own?"

"Sure. I have a savings account for college."

"All for college?"

"Well, it's my baby-sitting money."

"So go buy some jeans. I'll come with you after school today and we'll pick out a pair."

I looked at him in complete surprise. "Okay," I said. "I'll do it."

"See you after school, then. At the front gate."

"Okay," I said excitedly.

"You better get back to your friends now. They'll think you've totally flipped."

"No, they won't. See you after school, James."

"See ya, Karen."

I ran back to my friends.

"What was that all about?" Roni asked.

"Wasn't that the weirdo we saw the other day?" Justine asked, wrinkling her little nose.

"Weird Waldo," Ginger added helpfully.

"His name is James," I said firmly. "I don't like mean nicknames."

"Oh, I see, you're into social work now," Justine

said, grinning broadly. "You're going to attempt to re-habilitate social outcasts?"

"You better watch out, Karen. The guy could be a psycho," Ginger said.

"What's the matter with you people?" I snapped. "Just because someone chooses to dress differently doesn't mean that he's not a nice person. James happens to be a super guy, and I'm really glad I met him."

My friends were looking from me to each other with confused faces. "Karen, it sounds like you feel pretty strongly about him," Roni said. "I've never heard you yell before."

"I do feel strongly," I said. "Do you know why he dresses so strangely? Because all the kids made fun of him in elementary school—just for being smart. He started dressing differently to show that he didn't care what they thought. But he *does* care."

"Sounds like this is more than just social work," Justine commented. "You care, too, don't you?"

"Yes," I said. "I do. I really like him."

Justine put her hand on my arm. "Karen, he might be the nicest guy in the world, but if you want to fit in here, don't be seen hanging around with him. It doesn't take long to get a reputation. Trust me."

"I'm going to hang around with whoever I please," I said, jumping up from the grass. I grabbed my stuff and got ready to leave. Before I walked away, though, I turned back to my three startled friends. "I don't care what anyone thinks," I told them. "And if you can't be happy that I've met a guy I like, then you're not really my friends."

Chapter

10

My friends were waiting for me after our last class that afternoon. All afternoon, I had been ignoring them. Now they came up to me cautiously, as if I'd turned into a new and dangerous animal they weren't quite sure of.

"Karen, we didn't mean to upset you," Roni said.

"You did upset me," I answered flatly. "I didn't expect you, of all people, to judge someone by the way they look."

Roni's face flushed. "We just wanted to spare you from embarrassment," she said.

"Yeah, Karen, that weird guy could totally wreck your image," Justine said. "Believe me, I know how important image is."

Roni touched my arm. "I'd hate to see you get teased or hurt."

"I guess I'll have to get used to being teased," I said, "because I'm meeting James right now and we're going shopping together. I think I'm going to have fun with him. See ya later."

I didn't give them a chance to say any more. They might have apologized, but they still couldn't see my point of view. I tried to put them out of my mind as I went to find James.

He was waiting for me outside the school gates. "Onward. To the mall!" he said, dramatically flinging his cape back over his shoulders.

That afternoon I bought my first pair of jeans. I'd only meant to try them on, because I didn't have any money with me. But when I looked at my slim blue legs in the mirror, I really wanted them right away.

"Do you think I could put them on hold?" I whispered to him. "I don't have money with me. I have to go to the bank tomorrow and get some."

But James took out a checkbook and wrote a check. I was pretty impressed that anyone our age would have a checkbook, but I didn't feel at all comfortable as he started to write. "I can't let you pay for me," I said.

"Don't be a goofus," he said. "I've got the money.

And it's making you happy. I can see by your face that you're excited about this."

"Excited but scared," I said as he handed me the shopping bag. "I just hope there isn't going to be a big scene at home."

"What can they do?" he said. "You're not doing anything terrible. Sometimes you have to take a stand on things that are important to you. I did about my hair."

"Your parents didn't like it?"

"They freaked out over it, but I told them it was on my head, not theirs, and they'd have to get used to it."

"Wow, James. You really said that?"

He nodded and held open the door of the mall. We began walking slowly toward my house.

"I don't know if I'd ever have the nerve to say something like that," I said after thinking about it for a minute.

"Sure you would. Your parents can't expect to run your life forever." He grinned suddenly. "Tell you what—I'll come home with you, if you like, and help you tell them."

Horrified, I said, "Oh, no. Don't do that. I mean, I'd rather explain for myself. You don't know what my parents are like." Just the thought of my mother and James in the same room made me shudder.

"Whatever you say," he said. The smile had left his face. We came to a major intersection. "I go right here," he said flatly. I sensed I had done something to offend him, but I didn't know what.

"James, thank you so much for coming with me to get the jeans," I said. "And thank you for paying for them. I'll get you the money tomorrow afternoon, if you want to come with me after school."

"Sure. Okay." He gave me a hesitant smile.

"I'm so glad I met you," I told him. "I feel like I'm living a whole new life. It's exciting. I've never met anyone with the courage to be different before. You make me feel courageous, too."

He was looking at the ground, drawing circles with the toe of his shoe. "Karen, there's an exhibition of computer graphics and laser art at the museum. Would you like to go with me on Saturday . . . if you don't have anything better to do?"

"I'd love to, James," I said.

"Great." He was smiling again. "I'll find out what time the museum opens and all that stuff."

"Okay. See you at school tomorrow," I said.

"Good luck with the jeans," he called after me. "Be firm. Take a stand."

"I will."

I waved, and he waved back. Then I ran most of the way home.

My mother was in the kitchen as usual. I dumped my book bag down in the hall. "Hi, Mom," I called, inching my way into the bathroom. Before I lost my nerve, I pulled out my new jeans and put them on. Then I headed into the kitchen.

"How was your day?" she asked, pouring a glass of milk for me.

"Fine. How was yours?"

"Pretty busy," she said. "I was at church, getting ready for the harvest festival."

"Oh, that's right. It's this weekend, isn't it?" Every year the Vietnamese community at our church holds a big harvest celebration with traditional dances and food and games.

"This year I'm in charge of the stall with the pork buns and the cha gio," she said. "So I'm going to need some help."

Pork buns and Vietnamese egg rolls—why couldn't she get a less greasy stall? "How come you couldn't get the kite stall?" I asked. "Or the paper flowers?"

"Never mind what I could or couldn't get," she said calmly. "The fact is that I'm expecting you to help out."

"Is it all weekend?"

"Of course. Saturday and Sunday from eleven onward."

"Don't count on me to help. I've got plans for this weekend," I said.

She had been putting milk and cookies on the kitchen table. Now she looked up in surprise. "Plans? What plans? What sort of child makes plans without consulting her parents first? No more nonsense about camping trips, I hope?"

"No, nothing like that," I said. "A friend and I are visiting an exhibit at the art museum."

"Oh—a class project?"

"No, just something we're interested in."

"I didn't know you were interested in museums."

"It's computer graphics," I said.

"Computer what?"

"You make pictures with a computer. My friend has made this picture that turns over and over, just like it's coming out of the screen."

"Oh." She clearly didn't understand this. "Computer graphics, eh?"

"That's right."

"Since when are you interested in computers?"

"Since now. It's very clever, Mom. You should see it."

"Huh," she said. "Why would I want to see things going around and around on a screen?"

"It's the new direction of art. Pretty soon people won't paint on canvas anymore. They'll use programs to create pictures on computer screens."

"Huh," she said again. But the "Huh" turned into a squeak. "Karen! What have you got on your legs?"

I was tempted to say that my skin had turned into blue denim. Instead I took a deep breath and said, "Jeans."

"Jeans? Where did you get them?"

"At a store, like everyone else."

"You bought them?"

"Well, I didn't steal them!" I said with a lame smile.

"How did you pay for them?"

"I have money in my savings account," I said. I didn't think this was a good time to tell her a boy had bought them for me.

"But that's for college."

"Some of it's not. Some of it is birthday money and what I've made baby-sitting."

"You took money out of your account without asking your parents?"

"It's my money."

She made a sound like she was choking, as though she couldn't breathe because I'd dared to say something so terrible. I stood there, waiting for doom to fall—waiting to be sent to my room until I turned thirty. Instead she said, "Where is your skirt?"

"I took it off, Mom. It's in my bag."

"You plan to go outside, wearing those . . . blue jeans?"

"Yes, I do. Just like every other kid in the universe."

She came around the table to face me. I was taller than she was, but I was still scared. I could feel my heart hammering. "You disobeyed your parents and bought clothes we don't approve of," she said.

"Mom, I'm an American teenager and I bought clothes I like," I said. "Take a good look at them. There's nothing wrong with them. They are not indecent or cheap or anything that you could disapprove of. They're just normal jeans. See?"

I turned around to model for her.

"But they are not the correct clothes for school," she said at last.

"I don't go to a school that has a uniform anymore. Everyone else wears jeans and shorts. Only kids at Catholic schools wear pleated skirts."

"We should have kept you in the Catholic school, then," she said. "There they dress decently. The children at those schools are taught not to disobey their parents. You've become like the worst American teenager—you do exactly what you want without asking our permission! I'll talk to your father and see about sending you back to the Catholic school."

"You took me out of Catholic school because we

couldn't afford it anymore, remember?" I reminded her. "I'm having enough trouble fitting in at a public school without being teased about what I wear." I was thinking about James, not me. Nobody had actually laughed at me for wearing skirts every day, but she didn't have to know that.

She looked astonished. "They laugh because you're properly dressed?"

"I'm old-fashioned, Mom. Nobody wears a skirt except me."

She looked from my face to the jeans and back again. "I suppose they're not so bad," she said. "I can't see why you'd want to wear men's trousers, but they're not so bad."

I put my arms around her and hugged her. "Thanks, Mom," I said. "And you're not so bad, either."

She pushed me away, embarrassed. We didn't do much hugging in our family. "So much disrespect," she said, laughing. "What did we do to deserve a child like you?"

"You're pretty lucky," I said. "You should see some of the kids at my school."

"I've seen them," she said. "Boys with hair down past their shoulders! I blame their parents for not teaching them discipline at an early age. If one of them came near me, I'd scrub him and cut his hair with my sewing scissors."

I made a mental note to keep James away from my parents. "I can help you at your festival on Sunday," I said. "It's just Saturday I'm busy."

"That will be good," she said. "Sunday will be the busiest day. People stop by after church."

"I'll be there."

She nodded. "Drink your milk."

I grinned to myself as I had my milk and cookies. I'd had no idea that standing up to my mother would be so easy. I couldn't wait to tell James in the morning.

The next day I wore my jeans to school. My friends all did double takes as soon as I came through the door.

"Karen! What happened to your skirt?" Ginger cried.

"The skirt is gone," I said with a smile. "I've taken the first step on my road to independence."

"Way to go, Karen!" Roni yelled.

Even Justine looked impressed. "The jeans really fit well," she said. "They must have been expensive."

A little later, I was the one to get a surprise. James showed up at school in jeans and a white T-shirt. He still wore his big, clompy shoes and his hair in a ponytail, but apart from that, he looked totally mainstream. As soon as I could get him alone I grabbed his arm.

"Did you do this for me?" I asked.

"Do what?"

"Change your image?"

"Sort of. I thought you might need support from other jean wearers on your first day."

"You are so sweet," I said. "But you really don't have to change your image for me. I don't care how you dress."

"I don't want you to feel embarrassed with me," he said.

"Don't be silly. I like you just the way you are," I said.

"Honestly?" he asked, his eyes looking earnestly into mine.

I nodded. He smiled.

After school, James and I went to my bank and I paid him back. Then we sat on a wall behind the bank, just talking. It was amazing how much we had to talk about. I felt like I had known James all my life.

Chapter

11

When I told Roni, Justine, and Ginger about the computer art exhibition I was going to, I could see that they were bewildered. They couldn't understand why I was making such a big thing of going to a computer show with a guy they still thought of as Weird Waldo. Only Justine came right out and said anything, of course.

She took me aside as we left school on Friday afternoon. "Karen, let me give you a word of advice," she said. "It's no good getting new jeans if you're going to blow your image by being seen with that guy! Even Sean Baxter would have been a better choice."

"You still don't get it, do you?" I demanded. "I like

James. I like him the way he is. I'm happy when I'm around him. You should be happy for me."

"But are you sure you're not just doing this to make a statement?" she asked.

"What kind of statement?"

"You've been the perfect child until now. You've always done what your parents want. Maybe this is your version of rebellion. You bought jeans, and now you've chosen the most unsuitable boyfriend in the world. It's not unusual to go to extremes just to prove you're your own person."

"Like you do?" I asked.

"What do you mean?" she asked, nervously tossing back her ponytail.

"I mean the act you always put on, Justine," I said. "You know, when we were computer matching and you wanted a skydiving hunk who drove a Porsche and did all that other stuff. That was all phony. You were just scared that they would match you up with an ordinary guy."

She blushed crimson. "Okay, so maybe I do come on a little strong when I'm uncomfortable. I just wouldn't know what to do with an ordinary guy."

"But you don't have to pretend to be something you're not, Justine," I said. "We like you the way you are. And that's the way I feel about James. I don't care that he chooses to be different—that's just the way he is. I hope you have a chance to get to know him. Then you'd see what a sweet person he is and why I like him."

"I'm sure he's very nice," Justine said uncertainly. "It's just that you two don't have a thing in common. I mean, since when are you interested in computer art?"

"Since the moment I saw it," I said. "That's how James and I started talking, because I wanted to know more about it."

"I guess you know what you're doing, Karen," she said. "And there's no harm in going out in the middle of the afternoon—unless, of course, anyone from school sees you with him. But then, anyone who really matters wouldn't be seen dead at a computer art show. It would only be nerds."

"Justine!" I exclaimed.

She flushed again. "Sorry. I guess that was rude. Okay, so I need to stop my mouth from running away with me. I hope you have a nice time at your computer show. But just to be on the safe side, maybe you could go in through a side entrance?"

I couldn't help laughing. Justine wasn't going to change in a hurry. Image would always be important to her. Frankly, I didn't care who saw me. I no longer thought of James as weird at all. I liked the flamboyant way his cape swirled around him. I liked his ponytail and his interesting hat. He was like a character from a novel.

When I arrived at the art museum on Saturday morning, I couldn't spot James in the crowd of people standing on the steps, waiting for the museum to open. Then he came bounding down the steps toward me, his cape flowing out in the breeze, looking like a comic book hero. I wouldn't have been surprised to see him take off and fly.

"You came. I'm so glad," he said.

"I said I would."

"I thought you might change your mind."

"I wanted to come, you goofus," I said, using his term.

He smiled, and his whole face lit up. "Come on, then," he said. "Let's worm our way to the front of the line."

He took my hand and dragged me up the stairs. I hardly noticed the steps or the people. All I could think of was that James was holding my hand. I could feel the tingles going all the way up my arm. How could something so simple make me feel so incredible? I never wanted him to let go.

We made it to the front of the crowd and soon we were inside the exhibition. There were so many amazing things to see that we even forgot about holding hands. There was a room full of computer screens filled with such lifelike images that I could have sworn they were real. There was a room of holograms, including one of a full-size locomotive that steamed out of the wall.

When a hologram dinosaur turned its head in my direction, I grabbed James's arm. He looked down at me and grinned. "Just wait until you see the virtual-reality room," he said.

We got a chance to try a virtual-reality booth, and it was awesome. We put on these special glasses and creatures leaped out at us from all directions. They were so real that I jumped, and I ducked when a spear came hurtling toward me.

As we came out of the booth, we were laughing and still breathing hard. I could see that James, too, had been totally taken in by the game.

"Imagine having one of those in your den at home," he said. "Ten minutes with warriors from outer space would be a great escape from eight hours of school."

"Thanks, but I'll pass on that one," I said. "I was scared silly. But I wouldn't mind a virtual-reality booth where I could float down a river or go through a beautiful forest."

"You don't need *virtual* reality to do that. We'll do it for real sometime," James said. "My parents like to go hiking up in the country on weekends. I'll show you the most beautiful forest in the world." Suddenly he stopped, looking embarrassed. "That is, if you'd like to come with us," he finished quietly.

"I'd love to," I said. "I love the outdoors, but my parents are strictly stay-at-home types."

"Great," James said with a huge smile.

"I'm so glad you invited me to this art show, James," I told him. "It's been incredible. I never knew stuff like this existed."

"We could come back tomorrow," he said. We had crossed the marble foyer and emerged into bright sunlight.

"Oh, not tomorrow," I said. "I promised my mother I'd help her with her booth at our church festival."

"I'll help you if you like," he said easily. "I'm great at booths."

Alarm signals were going off in my head. There was no way I was ready for my parents to meet James. And I certainly didn't want him to see me, surrounded by pork buns, dressed in my traditional costume with Asian music wailing in the background.

"Oh, no, I don't think that would be a good idea," I said quickly.

"Why not? I don't mind," he said.

"I'll be too busy," I said, "and you wouldn't like it at all. It wouldn't be your kind of thing." I knew I was babbling. I saw the smile leave his face. His expression became guarded.

"I get it," he said.

"You get what?"

"You don't mind coming with me to something like this, because you know that nobody will see us together. But you don't want me to meet your family because I'd embarrass you. I thought you were different, Karen. I thought that at last I'd met someone really special, who didn't care . . ." He turned away from me and started down the steps. "Bye, Karen. See you around."

I stood like a statue on the steps, listening to the blood pound through my head. I felt like my throat had closed up—it was hard to breathe. I had hurt James, and all I'd wanted to do was save him from the embarrassment of meeting my parents. I'd never dreamed he'd feel that *he* was the one embarrassing *me*! I flew down the steps, practically pushing people out of the way.

"No, James, wait!" I yelled. "Don't go. Let me explain!"

But James didn't stop. I could see his cape swirling out behind him as he moved swiftly through the crowd. He was almost running now, into the gardens beside the museum. I ran, too. I could feel tears on my cheeks.

"James, please don't go!" I yelled.

The crowd closed in around me. When the path was clear again, James had disappeared. It was over. I had met a boy I really liked, and now he was gone.

Chapter

12

The next morning I got up and put on my yellow silk tunic with the long, peach-colored skirt underneath it. It felt strange and tight as I walked down to the kitchen, and I longed for my new jeans. I just hoped that the day would go quickly, so I could get back home and think about James. It was hard enough pretending I wasn't miserable in front of my parents—I was sure it would be even worse in front of all their friends at the festival.

My mother was in her traditional costume, too, her hair held up with combs and with a flower at one side.

"You look nice, Mom," I said as she handed me a pan of pork buns. "That outfit makes you look really young."

She looked surprised. Then she almost blushed. "Thank you, Karen."

"I bet you dressed like that when you went to festivals to meet boys," I said with a teasing grin.

"There wasn't much opportunity for festivals when I was your age," she said. "Always war. But I do remember once, during our spring festival . . . I was about your age. There was a wonderful dance with lanterns. Some girls and I performed the butterfly dance. It looked so pretty."

"And did you dance with boys, too?"

"A little," she said. "But the old people were always looking too closely."

I smiled. Maybe things hadn't changed so much after all. Except that I would never get to dance with a boy—or even go on a real date. I didn't want to date anyone but James, and James was gone. With a sigh, I followed my mother out to the car.

The festival always gave me a big case of déjà vu. The smells, the sounds, so many babies crying, so many little kids trying to fly kites. Ever since I was little, this festival had been exactly the same. All the people there said the same things every year—how proud my parents were of my violin playing, how I was growing into a fine young woman, how they hoped I'd stay away from all the bad American habits. I just put a fixed smile on my face and kept it there

146

while I handed out my pork buns and cha gio.

By the middle of the afternoon I was really hot. My silk costume felt sticky against my skin, and the steam from the pork buns was dripping off my face. But worst of all was the memory of my fight with James—I couldn't stop thinking about it. I had never been so unhappy.

A few Westerners strolled by our booth, but most of the people I served were Vietnamese. My mother was talking to one of her friends from church. I told her to take a walk around the other booths. I didn't mind serving the cha gio alone—after all, it kept my mind off James. But right after my mother left, a tall shadow fell across my booth.

"James!" I exclaimed, half in delight and half in horror. "What are you doing here?"

"I couldn't leave things the way they were," he said. "I heard an advertisement for the festival on National Public Radio. So I thought I would come see you. I'll leave if you want me to."

"No, don't go," I said quickly. I was thrilled that James was here. But at the same time I still didn't want him to see me like this—my face sticky with sweat and my thin silk clinging to my body. "I'm not really busy now," I told him, "so maybe we can talk."

"I was thinking about yesterday," James said, looking at the ground. "And I guess I can't be mad at you for being like everyone else. I suppose the way I look would make you embarrassed to be seen with me, especially in front of your parents."

"It's not like that at all, you goofus," I said. "It's the other way around. I was embarrassed for you to see me here."

He looked surprised. "Why?"

I shrugged. "Look at me—I look ridiculous! And my parents are here. They've forbidden me to date until I turn sixteen. I know they'd give you a hard time. I didn't want that."

He was looking at me so tenderly that I thought I'd melt.

"Forbidden you to date until you turn sixteen?" he repeated.

I nodded. "They're kind of old-fashioned."

"I'll say."

"And they're not very good with people they don't know. I didn't want you to feel uncomfortable."

"Are you going to obey them?" he asked, coming around my booth to stand next to me.

"You mean about not dating until I'm sixteen?"

He nodded.

"I suppose it depends on what you call dating," I said. "I could have guy friends."

"But what if a guy friend wanted to put his arms around you?"

"I could call that a friendly hug."

"I see." He slid his arms around my waist and pulled me close to him. "Like this?" he whispered. "This is a friendly hug, okay?"

"Okay," I whispered back. I could scarcely breathe, he was holding me so tight. Our faces were only inches apart.

"And a friendly kiss would be okay, too?" he asked.

Suddenly his lips were on mine. They were warm and gentle. Without thinking, I put my arms around his neck and kissed him back.

I had often wondered if I would know what to do when a boy kissed me. How would I know which way to tilt my head, how to position my lips, whether to close my eyes? Now it was happening to me, and it seemed like the most natural thing in the world. I didn't even care that we were in the middle of the Vietnamese festival and that lots of people could see us. All that mattered was James's lips on mine. I couldn't believe that anyone in the world had ever felt this way before.

When we finally broke apart we just stood there, gazing at each other. James was the one to break the silence.

"I don't think that counted as a friendly kiss," he said in a husky voice.

"It wasn't unfriendly," I said.

"I think you just disobeyed," he said, grinning down at me.

"I think I did, too. And you know what? I don't even care," I said. "I like you and I know that you're a nice person. If my parents can't accept you, then that's too bad. I mean, who else would want to kiss me while I'm wearing this outfit?"

James looked at me with interest. "You look great," he said finally. "That costume really suits you. You should wear it to school sometime."

"Are you out of your mind?"

"Why not? It looks terrific on you."

"You know what people are like at school."

"I bet they'd be interested," he said. "I bet they'd think you looked good."

"Maybe during Spirit Week, when they have all those crazy dress days," I said cautiously.

"Maybe to the homecoming dance," he said, equally cautiously, "with me."

"Maybe," I said. "I'd love to go to the homecoming dance with you, James, but I'm not promising to go in this costume. I'll have to see how brave I feel."

"So which do you recommend?" he asked.

It took a moment to realize he was talking about the food in front of me.

150

"The egg rolls," I said. "They've got shrimp in them."

"Okay. I'll try an egg roll." He took it. "Do I dip it in this sauce?"

"If you'd like to try a sauce made from dried fish and chilis."

"Sounds wonderful," he said, and made such a funny face that I laughed out loud.

"Not bad," he said. "It doesn't taste like dried fish. It tastes pretty good, in fact. Here, have a bite." He leaned across the counter and popped the egg roll into my mouth.

"Karen," came my mother's sharp voice, "what are you doing?"

I jumped back. I hadn't even heard her come up. What if she had seen me kissing James? "Um, I'm . . . serving a customer, Mom," I said weakly.

"A customer?"

"A friend from school."

I could see her taking in James's appearance. He wasn't wearing the cape today, but he still had on his big black hat and rainbow-colored suspenders.

"You're busy now. No time to talk to people from school," she said curtly.

James held out his hand. "Hi, Mrs. Nguyen. I'm James," he said. "Nice to meet you. Lovely festival you've got here."

Her face was like stone. She nodded. "Karen can't

151

talk now. She's busy working. Helping me," she said. "You'd better go now."

I touched his arm. "Why don't you take a stroll around and come back later, when I can take a break?" I said in a voice heavy with meaning.

He gave me a long look. "Are you sure?"

"I'm sure."

"Okay. Then maybe you can teach me dancing, Vietnamese style." He bent over and, before I could stop him, gave me a peck on the cheek.

I really wished he hadn't done that. I knew he had done it on purpose, so that my mother would see. But he wasn't the one who had to face her. As James walked away I took a deep breath and turned to my mother.

"That boy. You say he's a friend of yours?" she demanded.

"Yes, he is."

"Not the right sort of friend to have," she said. "Good thing your father wasn't watching. He wouldn't approve of a boy with hair like that."

"James is a very nice boy," I said. "Just because he chooses to dress differently doesn't make him a bad person."

"Only troublemakers dress like that," she said. "He was the one who told you to buy the jeans, I suppose?"

"He came with me to get them," I said.

"See? A troublemaker. You drop him right now, you understand? He'll be bad for your studies, bad for your music. Nothing but trouble."

"Mom, I'm not dropping him and he won't be bad for anything," I said, fighting to stay calm.

"You remember what your father said? No boys until you turn sixteen."

"Mom, I spend all day surrounded by boys," I told her.

"You know what I mean," she said. "No boyfriends. No dating. So don't get any ideas in your head about this boy, because your father will say no."

"Daddy can't stop me from meeting my friends at school," I said. "What is he going to do, lock me up?"

She looked around hastily. I suppose she was hoping that none of her Vietnamese friends heard me being rude to her.

"See? Already he's made you disrespectful," she said. "I knew that school wasn't a good idea. I'll talk to the principal at the Catholic school and see if they can give you some sort of scholarship."

"No!" I shouted. "I'm not leaving Alta Mesa. I like it. I like my friends."

"You'll go where your parents think is best for you," she said. "And if your friends look like that boy, then that is not the place for my child."

A crazy idea was growing like a bubble in my head. It was so monstrous that it made my heart race, but it just might work. I tried to face her calmly.

"If you don't let me stay at Alta Mesa and keep on seeing my friends, I'll never play the violin again," I said.

There was a horrible silence.

"You don't mean it," said my mother.

"I mean it. You can't force me to play the violin if I don't want to. And I won't."

I could see that I had struck a nerve. She realized that this was true—nobody could make me play the violin. They could put it in my hands, but they couldn't make me play.

"But you love the violin," she said weakly.

"Not as much as I love my school and my friends."

Another long silence.

She sat down on the chair behind the booth. "I don't know what the world's coming to," she said. "Daughters show no respect and disobey all the time . . ."

"You have to understand that you've got an American daughter," I said. "You've brought me up with good values. Now you have to trust me to use them. My friends are good people. James is very, very smart. His parents are college professors."

"College professors?"

"Yes, physics and anthropology."

"His mother, too?"

"Yes. She's the physics professor."

She shook her head and fanned herself with a napkin.

"And James is so smart that he doesn't go to regular classes. He's in gifted classes, or he works on his own."

She couldn't say anything to this, either.

"He's designing his own computer programs," I said. "He wants to go to Harvard or MIT."

I could see that she was crumbling—she'd had too many shocks in one afternoon. She stood up and began serving pork buns without saying another word.

A little later James showed up, clutching a dragon kite, his face glowing with excitement.

"Guess what? I won the kite-flying contest," he said.

My mother looked amazed. "You won?"

"I've always had a thing about kites," he said. "I showed them some tricks they didn't know."

"Karen says you're a very smart boy," my mother blurted.

"You have a very smart daughter, too," he said.

She nodded and smiled. "You want to take a break

now, Karen?" she asked. "Show your friend the puppets and the dancing?"

"Thanks, Mom," I said. "I'll be back soon."

I took James's hand and smiled up at him as we merged with the crowd.

13

On Monday morning I got to school early. I couldn't wait to tell my friends everything that had happened over the weekend. I couldn't wait to see James again, either. We'd had such a great evening together at the festival. We'd danced, just like my mother had done, beneath the lanterns. It had been magic.

The first people I bumped into in the hall were the nerds. I was about to hurry past, but Owen yelled out to me, "Hey, Karen! Were you at the computer graphics exhibition this weekend?"

If I'd wanted to keep it secret, Owen would have totally blown it. Now the whole hall knew.

"Yes," I said cautiously. I know Justine would have denied it, but I couldn't.

157

"See," Owen said excitedly to Ronald and the other nerds, "I told you it was her." He turned to me. "We had no idea you were into computers in a big way. That's amazing."

"You'll be the first female member of our Computer Club," Walter said, blinking excitedly. "I can't wait to induct you on Wednesday."

"Oh, uh, thanks, but I don't know anything about computers," I said. "I only went because my friend is into them."

"Then it's true," Owen squeaked. "You were with that Waldo guy. We saw it, but I said, 'No, not Karen. She wouldn't want to be seen with a weird person like that.'"

I was trying not to laugh. Here I was in a main hallway, surrounded by occupants of the twilight zone, and they were worried about my being seen with James!

"You better get used to it, guys," I said. I would have told them about James's brilliant computer art, but then they'd try to force him into their club, and I knew he wouldn't like that. Luckily we were standing next to the girls' bathroom. "Gotta go," I said, and popped inside. Only one person was in there— Ginger.

"Hi," I said. "Where's Roni?"

She looked at me coldly. "You mean she hasn't

called you this morning to tell you her exact movements?"

"What?" I asked. I went over and perched on the edge of the sink. "Ginger, have I done something to upset you? Because I get the feeling that you're mad at me, and I don't know why."

"Forget it," she said.

"No, I don't want to forget it," I said. "We've all noticed that you've been acting strange. The other two think that something at home or with Ben is upsetting you, but I get the feeling that it's me you're mad at—and I can't understand why."

"I don't want to talk about it," she said. She picked up her bag and tried to walk past me.

I grabbed her arm. "Look, Ginger. You have to talk about it," I said. "You can't go on being eaten up inside. I'm your friend. It hurts me to see you like this. Especially if there's anything I can do to make you feel better. Please tell me."

She looked at me. Her freckled face was bright red. "It sounds so childish," she said, "and I know it's not your fault."

"What's not my fault?" I let go of her.

"That Roni likes you better than me," she blurted.

This took me totally by surprise. "Roni likes me better? What on earth gave you that idea?"

"She hardly even talks to me on the bus going

home now. And she spends all her evenings talking to you. You two seem so close, it scares me."

"Scares you? Why?"

"Because Roni and I have been best friends since kindergarten. I don't want to lose her."

"Ginger, why would you lose her?" I said gently. "Just because Roni is someone who understands what I've been going through at home doesn't mean that she won't have time for you anymore." I shook my head. "You have to understand, Ginger. It's been so wonderful to have Roni to talk to. She knows what it's like to have parents who make weird rules and don't let you act like a normal person. But I'm not trying to take her away from you. You two will always have a special relationship, because you've known each other for so long."

"I'm sorry, Karen," Ginger said, looking away from me. "Jealousy is so dumb, but I couldn't help myself. It's always been just the two of us until now."

"I guess high school is the time for branching out and making lots of new friends," I said. "I know it is for me."

"Look, you won't mention this to the others, will you?" she asked.

"I think we should talk about it, Ginger," I said. "We've all been worried about you. We've known something's wrong, and we haven't known how to help."

Ginger laughed nervously. "So that's what that dumb psychologist stuff was all about when we slept over at Justine's! Boy, talk about subtle."

I laughed, too. "I know, it was pretty bad, but we were trying to get you to tell us what was bugging you."

Ginger smiled shyly. "You guys were nice to put up with me. I know I've been a pain lately."

"It's okay. I understand. And I know Roni will want to set things straight with you. She cares a lot about you, Ginger. She's always saying how lucky she's been to have you for a friend."

"She said that?"

I nodded. "Come on, let's go find the others," I said.

She gave me a little hug. "Thanks, Karen."

As we walked out into the hallway, I heard a loud yell. Roni and Justine were running toward us, mowing down students around them.

"Wait till you hear what happened!" Roni yelled.

"I knew that stupid computer nerd got it all wrong!" Justine yelled.

People were looking at them and at us.

"And we actually want these people for friends?" I muttered to Ginger. She grinned.

Roni and Justine reached us, panting.

"Okay, tell us before you explode," Ginger said.

161

"Drew asked me to the homecoming dance," Roni said. "Imagine, me at the homecoming dance with Drew! It's like a miracle. Somebody pinch me . . . ow! Justine, I didn't really mean that."

"So the stupid program was wrong," Justine added. "But just about Drew and Sean. I bet if the nerds ran a real program for me, they'd come up with a long list of cute guys who were exactly my type." She turned to me. "They should rerun the program for you, too, Karen."

"No, thanks," I said. Wait until they heard the details of my weekend!

"I'm happy for you, Roni," Ginger said. "I'm glad things worked out okay with you and Drew."

Roni nodded. "Yeah, I know I haven't been very easy to get along with recently. I've hardly talked to you on the bus going home. But I was so scared that I'd lost Drew, I couldn't think about anything else."

"You see, Ginger?" I asked.

Roni and Justine looked at us curiously. "Ginger was scared that you and I were getting to be best friends and that we were shutting her out," I explained.

Roni looked amazed. "So all this time you thought I had deserted you?"

Ginger was examining her sneaker. "That's what it seemed like to me."

"You should have told me," Roni said. "We've never kept things from each other before."

"I felt stupid," Ginger said. "I knew I was being childish, but I couldn't stop myself."

"At last we unlock the mystery," Justine said. "If you guys would only learn to say what you think, like me, none of this would've happened. Being honest is one of my better qualities, I think."

Roni, Ginger, and I glanced at each other and grinned.

"What?" Justine said defensively.

"Nothing," Roni and Ginger said in unison. I didn't say anything. I had just noticed a familiar cape flowing through the hallway. James was walking in my direction.

"Oh, no, here comes Waldo," Justine hissed, loudly enough for half the hall to hear.

"His name is James," I reminded her. "You'd better get that straight now, because you're going to be hearing a lot of it in the future."

"So what happened over the weekend?" Roni demanded. "How was the computer show?"

James had drawn even with us. "I'm not going to put this in your locker this time," he said, and he handed me a perfect pink rose.

"Can I walk you to class?" he asked.

I took his hand. "I'll tell you all the details at

lunchtime," I called back to my friends. Then I walked away down the hall with James's hand in mine, leaving the Boyfriend Club staring open-mouthed behind me.

About the Author

Janet Quin-Harkin has written over fifty books for teenagers, including the best-seller *Ten-Boy Summer*. She is the author of the *Friends* series, the *Heartbreak Café* series, and the *Senior Year* series. She has also written several romances.

Ms. Quin-Harkin lives with her husband in San Rafael, California. She has four children. In addition to writing books, she teaches creative writing at a nearby college.

Here's a sneak preview of
The Boyfriend Club™ #4:

Queen Justine

You know how people can always tell you exactly what they were doing when a disaster struck? I mean, people remember the song that was playing on the radio when there was an earthquake—things like that. Well, I can tell you exactly what I was doing on the Friday that changed my life.

I had just arrived home from school and I was vegging out with a bowl of macadamia nut ice cream, watching a rerun of *The Beverly Hillbillies* and wondering why they didn't hire a wardrobe consultant with all that money. I was enjoying having the house to myself for once. My stepmother, the wicked witch, was out somewhere with my dad. I knew she was due back soon, because they were having guests over for dinner. So I was making the most of curling up in her new pink silk armchair and watching the giant-screen TV instead of the little set in my bedroom.

On the way home from Alta Mesa, I had tried not to think about the fact that I was skipping Pride Day the next day. My friends had been sort of cold to me when we'd said good-bye after school. Maybe they thought I was letting them down by not taking part. But I really didn't want to spend my weekend picking up trash. I could understand why they were so eager to do it. If I had a cute boyfriend like Drew, it might have been fun to throw around paint with him. If I had a guy like Ben, we could have talked while we picked up trash. Even if I had a guy like James, I'm sure I could have *some* fun. But I had nobody. I'd have to spend the entire day watching my friends with their boyfriends, while I was all alone.

I thought about this again as I sat curled in the witch's chair. I wasn't special to anyone in the world! Not to a boy, and certainly not to my father and the wicked witch. I turned up the TV even louder. So loud, in fact, that I didn't hear the front door open.

The first hint I had that anybody had come in was the voice screeching behind me. "Justine, are you watching TV in the family room? You better not be eating in there."

Hastily I shoved my bowl of ice cream under the

chair as the wicked witch walked in. I have to point out, in all fairness, that she doesn't look like a witch. She is actually very beautiful—tall, slim, not a hair out of place, great taste in clothes. I can see why my father fell for her. But just because she looks good doesn't mean she's any less of a witch. In fact, her pretty blue eyes looked at me now with an icy glare.

"Turn that down, Justine," boomed my father's voice right behind me. I turned down the sound.

"Why do you have to have it so loud?" my stepmother demanded. "It can't be good for your ears. Two seconds of it was giving me a splitting headache!"

"And you do have your own set in your room," my father pointed out. "Why can't you watch that?"

"Fine. Banish me to my room," I snapped. "I feel more like Cinderella every day. You'll have me scrubbing the floor and wearing rags next."

I started out of the room, but my stepmother touched my father's arm. "No, Jack, that's not right," she said. "Don't make her feel unwanted in her own house. Of course she's welcome to watch TV down here when we're not around."

"Yeah, right," I snapped. "Everything's fine as long as I stay out of your hair."

"Justine, that's not fair," my stepmother began, but my father cut in.

"Justine, I won't have you being rude to Christine. She's trying very hard to get along with you. And she doesn't need any upsets in her life right now."

"It's okay, Jack," Christine said sweetly.

"No, it's not okay. I don't want you under any stress," he said to her. "In fact, shouldn't you be sitting down? Why don't I get you a cool drink?"

"Is Christine sick?" I demanded. She was acting all cutesy as my father helped her to the sofa.

"You're so sweet," she said, giggling. "I'm perfectly okay, Jack, honestly. Women in China go on working in the fields until the ninth month."

I heard what she was saying, but my brain wouldn't accept it. It couldn't be possible. My father already had gray hair! He was . . . well, elderly. And she wasn't young, either. She spent a fortune on anti-wrinkle creams and spa treatments.

"Wait a minute," I said, interrupting their giggling. "Did I hear right? Are you saying that Christine's going to have a baby?"

Two excited faces looked up at me. "That's right, princess," my father said. "We just came back from the doctor's office and it's official. You're going to be a big sister. Isn't that wonderful?"

I stared at them as coldly as I dared. "Two old people like you? I think it's disgusting," I said. I ran across the marble entrance hall and up the stairs. I could hear my father yelling to me and Christine saying, "Let her go, Jack. This has been a shock for her." But I didn't stop until I was safely in my room.

I closed the door and flung myself down on my bed, gathering my stuffed animals into my arms and burying my face in their soft fur. When Dad had announced that he was marrying Christine, I thought it was the very worst thing that could ever happen to me. For all those years we'd just had each other. Oh, I know he'd always been busy, but whenever he came to my school and took me out for the day, he tried his hardest to give me a good time. He took me to expensive stores and let me buy whatever I wanted. He always called me his princess.

But now he had a new princess, someone he liked better than me. And he would definitely like his new child better than me. I could picture how it was going to be: Everybody fussing over a dumb baby, and the kid allowed to touch all my old toys and mess up my room, and nobody giving two hoots if I was alive or not.

I lay there for a long time, hugging Teddy Blue and Panda and Hump-free Bogart, my camel, breathing in their familiar smell and feeling the fake fur tickle my face. I needed someone to hug me back, someone who was alive and cared about me. Suddenly I realized something: I had friends now. I could call up Roni and Ginger and Karen, and they'd care. They'd know how to make me feel better.

I reached across to my bedside table and picked up the phone. I called Karen first. I was sure she'd understand. After all, she was an only child, too.

The phone rang several times. Then a voice said hesitantly, "Hello. Who is this, please?"

I remembered Karen had told me that her mother hated answering the phone.

"Hi, it's Justine," I said. "Is Karen there?"

"Oh, Justine, hello," she said, her voice softening. "Sorry. Karen is not here. She's with James. They're going to a movie."

"Oh," I said. "Will you ask her to call me if she doesn't get home too late?"

"Very well. I'll tell her," Mrs. Nguyen said. "Goodbye Justine." Then she hung up.

I fought back my disappointment that Karen wasn't around when I needed her. That dumb James was taking up all her time now. I dialed Roni's number.

"Please be there. Please answer," I prayed. Her voice came on the line. "Roni?" I almost yelled. "It's Justine."

"Oh, hi, Justine. What's up?"

"Guess what," I began, "I just found out that my stepmother's going to have a baby—"

"No kidding? That's great, Justine. I'm so happy for you. You'll have so much fun taking care of a little baby!" She didn't give me time to say anything. "I remember how sweet Paco was when he was just born. I'm glad you called to tell me, but I've got to go. Drew's playing football tonight. I have to go cheer him on. See you tomorrow, Justine."

Then she hung up, leaving me feeling like a deflated balloon. How could she think I'd be happy with something like a baby? I mean, I like babies in theory, but not in my house and not when the baby is going to take my place! I was about to call Ginger when I remembered that if Roni was going to watch Drew play football, then Ginger would be going to watch Ben. She wouldn't have time for me, either. It really was true: I had nobody who cared about me.

You don't need
—— a boyfriend to join! ——

Now you and your friends can join the real Boyfriend Club and receive a special Boyfriend Club kit filled with lots of great stuff only available to Boyfriend Club members.

- **A mini phone book for your special friends' phone numbers**
- **A cool Boyfriend Club pen**
- **A really neat pocket-sized mirror and carrying case**
- **A terrific change purse/keychain**
- **A super doorknob hanger for your bedroom door**
- **The exclusive Boyfriend Club Newsletter**
- **A special Boyfriend Club ID card**

All this for just $3.50!

If you join today, you'll receive your special package and be an official member in 4-6 weeks. Just fill in the coupon below and mail to: The Boyfriend Club, Dept. B, Troll Associates, 100 Corporate Drive, Mahwah, NJ 07430

☐ **Yes, I want to be a member of the real Boyfriend Club. I have enclosed a check or money order for $3.50 payable to The Boyfriend Club.**

Name_____

Address_____

City_____State_____Zip_____

Age_____Where did you buy this book?_____

Sorry, this offer is only available in the U.S.

ADVICE EXCHANGE

Boyfriend Club Central asked:

What should you do when you want to date but your parents say you're not old enough?

And you said:

I have more fun with my girl friends than with any of the boys I've dated.

- Liz M., Los Angeles, CA

Ask your parents if you can date in groups.

- Bonnie S., Harrisburg, PA

Keep asking your parents when you can date. Maybe they'll change their minds.

- Lisa N., Buffalo, NY

Invite the person you want to date to your house to meet your parents.
- Amy W., Greensboro, NC

Tell your parents that all your friends are dating.
- Pam A., Houston, TX

Have fun with your friends for now and wait until your parents say you can date.
- Kristy M., Morristown, NJ

Invite your friends and the boy you like to your house for a party.
- Kelly P., Rye, NY

Now we want to know:
What can you do to make new friends when you're the new kid in school?

Write and tell us what you think, and you may see your advice in a future ADVICE EXCHANGE:

Boyfriend Club Central
Dept. B
Troll Associates
100 Corporate Drive
Mahwah, NJ 07430